"Do you think we're trying too hard?"

Abe looked into her eyes. "I can't say, Anna. I just know I'm very sad inside and I see it in you, too. I don't think our mates would want us to always be so unhappy and lonely. I'm not looking for love. Not yet, anyway. It's too soon, but I am looking for a woman who is kind enough to care for my *kinner*. My little Alice—Allie—needs a *mudder* real bad. And your *buwe*? Do you think they'd do better with a man in the house?"

She nodded as she looked down at the tablecloth. "They don't listen to me. I don't know if they'd listen to anyone, but sometimes I feel frustrated by my failings as a *mudder*."

"You're not failing them, Anna. I know you love them and try your hardest. *Kinner* need parents. Both a *mudder* and a *daed*. You're the first woman I've met who I think I could care about. I mean really care. Someday…"

June Bryan Belfie has written over twenty-five novels. Her Amish books have been bestsellers and have sold around the world. She lives in Pennsylvania and is familiar with the ways of her Amish neighbors. Mother of five and grandmother of eight, Ms. Belfie enjoys writing clean and wholesome stories for people of all ages.

AWAKENING LOVE

June Bryan Belfie

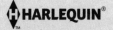

Recycling programs
for this product may
not exist in your area.

ISBN-13: 978-1-335-08146-9

Awakening Love

Copyright © 2015 by June Bryan Belfie

Printed in U.S.A.

Chapter One

Anna took her friend's baby in her arms while Dinah turned the bacon. The wonderful odor of bacon and coffee permeated the small Amish kitchen as the meat sizzled merrily in the iron pan. Dinah turned and laid the spatula on a dish and folded her arms. She cocked her head and grinned at her friend. "So you are going to Abe's for the whole afternoon?"

"Yah, and for supper, too." Anna couldn't hold back her own smile. She had barely slept the night before. Perhaps taking this trip to visit her friend in Ohio had been a God thing. It certainly was odd that she had been praying for Abe Stoltzfus all these months and then he suddenly turned up in her life—just when she felt the need to move on from her own days of mourning. Who would have thought the article she read in the bulletin about the tragic buggy accident, which took the lives of Abe's wife and three of his children, would end up with her actually meeting him.

"I can't believe you and Abe hit it off so well. He's

been introduced to a dozen young women in the last several months and nothing ever came of it."

"I guess he wasn't ready to consider anyone in his life at that point."

"Maybe, but I think Gott was waiting till Abe was ready and then sent you here on purpose."

"Oh, Dinah, what if he does want to marry me? What should I say?"

"Mercy, that's not something I can answer. You mentioned needing a man to father the boys. It doesn't have to be love, you know."

"I know." Baby Hannah began wiggling and sucking air with her sweet full lips. "I think your boppli needs to be nursed."

"That's all she does. I think she's going through a growing spurt. Will you take over the breakfast? The bacon is nearly done."

"Sure." Anna rose and handed the swaddled baby to her friend, who sat on the vacated chair to nurse her child. Anna removed the bacon and placed it on a paper towel over a plate. "How many eggs should I cook?"

"Oh, at least half a dozen. Maybe eight. Hosea comes in about now for his main breakfast. He had oatmeal and toast earlier. The man can eat like a horse."

"Jah, but he needs to. Look how hard he works."

"That's for sure."

After breaking the fresh eggs into the fry pan, Anna began cutting the homemade wheat bread for toast. She glanced over at Dinah, who was smiling down at her baby. It was a beautiful picture. One she'd given up happening ever again in her own life. Until yesterday.

"I miss suckling an infant," Anna said. "New boppli are so dear."

"Jah, they are. You're young, Anna, you still have time for more."

"It does take a man, you know," she said, grinning.

"I know one," joked her friend.

"I'm nervous, Dinah. What if he doesn't like me? And what if his children don't either?"

"Why would you even think that? You're one of the sweetest women I know. Everyone likes you."

"You say that because you're my best friend."

"Nee, I say that because it's true! Even Hosea says you're a really nice person."

"I just hope it goes well later. I'm going to wear my church dress. Do you think he'll notice it's the same one?"

"Men don't notice what frack we wear. Goodness, that's silly to even think about."

"My prayer kapp got wrinkled yesterday."

"Anna, relax. Just go and be yourself. Maybe it won't end in a permanent relationship, but you might have fun for a change. Maybe that's enough right now."

"You're absolutely right. It will just be gut to get with people. I've really enjoyed my visit so far. I hope I'm not in the way. Should I flip the eggs or leave them sunny up?"

"Flip six of them for Hosea. I already ate an hour ago. The other two are for you."

"I don't know if I can eat right now. My tummy is doing flips."

"You'd better eat something or you could faint."

Anna laughed. "I'll try. What about the toast?"

"Hosea eats four pieces. I do them in the fry pan for him when the eggs are out. He likes the grease."

"It's bad for you."

"Tell him that. He'd eat nothing but meat and eggs if I let him. I have to push the veggies on him."

"You're a gut wife, Dinah. I think he knows that you do it to help him. I love to see the way he looks at you. Like so full of love and all. I miss that."

"I'm sure you do. It's been real hard on you, ain't it?"

"Oh jah. You have no idea. Jeremiah was a wonderful-gut man. The best. I feel guilty even thinking about…"

"He's gone to a better place, Anna. He'd want you to be happy—and the kinner. You know that."

Anna sighed as she placed the cooked eggs on a plate and arranged the bread in the pan. "I guess."

"Nee, I *know* he'd want you to marry again. Jeremiah was not a selfish person. He'd expect you to re-marry."

"I need to tell myself that." She turned the flame up on the bread and stared at the pan.

"Hannah's fallen asleep already. She's a fast eater. Let me put her down in her cradle by the fireplace and I'll get Hosea in for his breakfast. He said he'd be in the barn."

After laying the baby down, Dinah rang the large bell attached to the back porch post, and within minutes, her husband was in the kitchen. He hung up his jacket and ran his hands in hot water. "So I hear you're going over to Abe's," he said, grinning over at Anna as he reached for a towel.

"Goodness, I hope the whole community isn't aware of our date. I mean get-together."

"Everyone has been praying for a woman to come into Abe's life, Anna. He's had a rough time of it. I'm thinking you might be the one." He sat at the table and Dinah placed his breakfast in front of him and filled a mug with coffee. He nodded and then silently said grace.

As they sat together they talked about the church service and the message about forgiveness, which was so often preached. Anna checked the clock on their mantle. It was only nine in the morning. Five hours before Abe would be coming to pick her up. Goodness that was a long time to wait.

"Let me help you with the wash," she said as Hosea prepared to leave for the barn again.

"I have the diapers soaking down in the basement already," Dinah said.

"I'll go finish them up and then run them through the ringer for you."

"You are a doll, Anna. That way maybe I can get dinner started. I want to make a pot roast today. I thought you'd be here—"

"Oh, Dinah, I'm sorry. I didn't even think to ask about your plans."

"Nee, don't even mention it. I'm thrilled you're going to Abe's place. We'll eat it at noon and then have the left-overs tonight for supper. It's not important."

Anna tried to put guilt out of her mind yet again. She hated displeasing anyone, but Dinah seemed sincere about the whole thing. Guilt was a strong emotion. Hopefully, through prayer and the words of her friends, she'd be able to get past that. Otherwise, a marriage would be impossible. It wouldn't be fair to anyone if she walked around feeling guilt all day. She had been totally faithful to her husband when he was living. There was no reason for her remorse. She knew it intellectually, yet emotionally, it would take more time. And prayer.

Around half past twelve, Anna took a sponge bath and put on her favorite dress. Maybe men didn't really notice, but she felt good in her green dress. It fit her perfectly and the color picked up the green in her eyes. Was she being vain? Mercy, it wouldn't do for an Amish widow to be vain about her looks. Oh dear, there was that guilt again! She shook her head, inwardly scolding herself, and then reached for her shawl. Hopefully, even if this didn't end in a long term relationship, she could make his children happy for the day. Apple dumplings always went over well in her home. Not many children turned away from dessert.

She went downstairs and sat anxiously waiting for Abe to arrive. Dinah patted her on the shoulder. "One thing about Abe you should know. He's always on time for everything. He expects that from everyone else, too."

"Gut. I like promptness in a man and I'm always ready early." She checked the time and it was five minutes to one. In the distance, she heard a buggy coming down the gravel drive. Oh my, she was nervous indeed.

Chapter Two

Josiah Yoder no longer smiled as he worked. His elation over forming a new relationship with a woman he loved, was gone. So was she. Oh, she still came in on workdays and did her job in his wood-working shop by handling the customers in the showroom. She still answered his questions—which were few and far between—but it was strained.

The wonderful moments on Christmas Eve day when he held Beth in his arms ever so briefly and exchanged the sweetest kiss of his life, were tarnished indelibly by her gift to him. Nee, not to him. To an Englisher—a handsome, successful man obviously smitten with the woman he loved and she in turn thought enough of the man to knit gloves for him. And then when that seemed to not work out, she turned around and gave those gloves to him! What made him think she'd made them for him in the first place?

What a fool he'd been. Nee, he'd remain single. That was his plan. That way you can't get hurt. His earlier relationship with another woman years before had ended in a disaster. Would he never learn? He loved his carpentry. Well, he used to. Nothing seemed to bring him joy anymore. He'd even pictured himself the father of many kinner. It wasn't meant to be. Gott had other plans, that was for sure and certain.

He heard the front door as Beth made her way in to start the day. She nodded his way and he acknowledged her presence by nodding back, and then he turned toward the cabinet he was staining.

It was slow. Perhaps he should have closed from Christmas through the New Year's, but he'd hoped for some business. And maybe he didn't want so many days to go by without seeing Beth. Was he that foolish to put himself in such a vulnerable position to be hurt again—and again?

Lunchtime rolled around and Beth came back to the workshop to pour herself some water.

"No customers yet?" he asked, continuing to apply the dark oak finish to a set of cabinets he was working on.

"Nope."

"Hmm."

"Josiah, I've been thinking."

He looked over and saw her expression. Her brows creased as she licked her lips.

"Go on."

"I'm giving you my notice. I'd like to be done within a week."

"I see." He cleared his throat and placed his brush on the counter and folded his arms as he leaned against the wall. "Do you want more money?"

Beth let out a disgruntled sound. "You know that's not the reason. Don't play games with me."

"I wasn't the one playing games."

"That hurts."

"Sorry." He pulled on his suspenders as he scuffed the toe of his shoe on the floor.

"I don't believe you are. You never gave me a chance to even explain about the note you found."

"What's to explain? You worked hours on making those gloves and apparently the recipient didn't appreciate all your efforts. Did you have a quarrel with your English sweetheart?"

"Don't be ridiculous! We were never more than friends."

"I don't believe that for a minute, Beth."

"It's true."

"But you wanted it to be more, didn't you? You hoped he'd fall madly in love with you and propose marriage and you'd leave the Amish and live a high old life!"

"Okay, for a while I was sort of infatuated with him. I admit that. But I knew down deep it wouldn't work out for us."

"Then why the gloves? Was he too poor to buy some for himself?"

"I just thought it would be nice to—"

"Don't go on any further. Sure, you can leave your job. Anytime. Today can be your last day. It's slow right now." He walked over to his desk and removed his checkbook and opened it to a fresh check. "I'll pay you for the whole week."

"That's not necessary."

"Oh, but it is. I wouldn't want word to get around that I cheated you."

"Abe, don't." In spite of her attempts, tears began to flow down her cheeks. "This isn't the way I wanted things."

"Nor I, Beth. Nor I. I really thought I'd met the woman of my dreams."

"Please, don't say that. I feel so terrible. You don't know how much I really care for you, Josiah."

"Please spare me." He scribbled on the check and tore it from the book, practically throwing it at her. Then he stomped across the room and walked out the back door, slamming it behind him.

Beth held the check in her hands and continued to weep. What had she done? She'd come so close to having what every Amish woman dreams of—a husband, a home, security. And love.

It was over. Completely. And they couldn't even remain friends. Not after everything that had transpired. She wished she'd never met Randy Gordon. He wasn't half the man Josiah was. He'd been after her for one reason only. And here he was even engaged! What a loser!

Nee, she was the loser. Her vanity had brought this upon her. She had thought Randy saw her as a woman—a potential mate even, while the whole time he was playing games with her. And she had allowed him to kiss her! And she'd even enjoyed it!

She deserved to be miserable. What a failure. And on top of that, she'd given up her job teaching to be with Josiah. Now she had nothing. No job—no beau—nothing.

She crumpled the check in her hand and threw it

on his desk. Then she grabbed her shawl and headed towards her buggy. After harnessing the horse, she made her way towards the road. A slap of the whip in the air alerted the horse to her desire to move quickly, and the horse began to gallop home.

Josiah watched from behind a shed as the woman he loved broke his heart and galloped out of his life—forever.

Abe glanced over at his passenger, admiring her classical profile. Anna Miller had come into his life out of the blue. Was she an angel in disguise? When he'd given up all hope of finding a mate and a mother for his children, she had suddenly appeared—and she knew of him! And had been praying for them—by name! What a miracle.

"Are you warm enough?" he asked as she stared straight ahead. She turned and nodded.

"Oh jah. Sure. You have a fine buggy."

"Denki. It's pretty cozy."

"Is it new?"

His expression changed from one of happiness, to one of sadness.

Of course it was new. How careless of her to ask. Their other buggy had been destroyed in the accident. Oh, she wished she could take back her words.

"I'm sorry. I wasn't thinking," she said softly as she turned back to look out the front window.

"It's okay. The old one was larger. I didn't need such a large one this time." They were silent for the rest of the ten minute ride. When he pulled up to his farmhouse, two little heads popped up in the front window.

John and Benny grinned at them and then ran to the front door to open it.

Abe laughed. Anna felt herself relax from her faux pas. "They're so cute. They look like their daed," she added.

"Jah, that's what I'm told. And Allie is the spitting image of their mamm."

"Will she be here today?"

"Later, my schwester will bring her over to play. I think she wants to see more of you, too." His smile was crooked as he held his hand for her. She climbed down from the buggy.

"Denki." It was nice to have a man's attention. He seemed very mannerly. His hand was warm on hers. She liked it.

As they came through the front door, Anna looked around. The house was clean, but a bit untidy, with a few clothes lying about and several board games in process, on tables and the floor. Apparently, Abe didn't pay much attention to details. But what man does? It was a bright house with large windows, unadorned by curtains or drapes. Very plain. The sofa was dark brown and showed signs of wear. There were three straight back chairs against one wall and a small wind-up clock on an end table by the sofa.

"Do you want to see the puzzle we're working on?" John asked, even before she had her shawl off.

"Now boys, Anna and I are going to have kaffi first. Then maybe we'll play a game together. Okay?"

The child's eyes showed such disappointment, Anna felt compelled to say something. "I'd love to help with your puzzle, but not yet." She looked over at Abe who reached for her shawl. "Do you do puzzles, too?" she asked as she handed it over.

"Nee, I'm terrible at them. Mary…their mamm liked to help them."

"I see. Sometimes they're too hard for me, too."

"Not me," John said, proudly. "I'm real gut at puzzles. Ask Benny."

Benny nodded in agreement. "He's much better than I am."

"But you're gut at the edges," John said.

Benny smiled. "Jah, pretty gut. I can play monopoly too."

"Oh, that's ever so much fun," Anna said, smiling at the two boys. What a difference she saw already in their behavior from her own children. Her boys would be fighting over the puzzle instead of working together. How would Abe handle that?

Once in the kitchen, Abe motioned for her to sit at the long trestle table centered in the large room. "I made the kaffi earlier. I hope it's not too strong." He brought it over to the table and set it on a tile.

"I like it any way you make it," she said, licking her lips. She looked around at this room—the heart of every Amish home. The place families gathered for meals and friends came for advice or sympathy. It was Mary's and she no longer could be there. A lump formed in Anna's throat. This would never work.

"Do you take cream?" Abe was asking as she came out of her thoughts.

"Jah, if you have any," she said.

"Oh, jah, I'm a dairy farmer, you know." He grinned.

"Oh, that's right. I remember now. Dinah told me that. How many cows do you own?"

"Only twenty right now."

"We used to have a dozen, but when my husband passed away, it was too much for me. My bruder took all but one. He makes sure I always have enough milk though for my kinner. He's a gut bruder."

"He sounds like it." Abe set a small pitcher of cream on the table and sat across from her on a bench. "Do you like my big kitchen?" he asked.

"Oh, jah, very nice. I bet you can cook for lots of people in here."

"Jah, Mary was a gut cook." He looked down at his mug and stirred in some sugar. "Do you like to cook, Anna Miller?"

She grinned. It sounded funny to hear him say her whole name. "I used to. Lately, everything has been a struggle."

"I know. Me too."

"Do you cook, Abe?"

"Not if I can help it. So far, between neighbors and family, I've had to cook very little. The boys like hot dogs, so we eat them a lot. And venison burgers. I haven't made stew in a while, but I'm pretty gut at that. Just throw stuff in and boil it."

She looked over and smiled. "I'm anxious to try it."

"You might be sorry you said yes," he said, grinning back.

"Do you want me to start the apple dumplings yet?" she asked.

"You have plenty of time. Let's just get to know each other better."

"It seems strange to be sitting here with a man who I hardly know, in a kitchen and all."

"I know." He looked down and turned his mug several times. "It's not easy."

"Do you think we're trying too hard?" she asked unexpectedly.

He looked into her eyes. "I can't say, Anna. I just know I'm very sad inside and I see it in you, too. I don't think our mates would want us to always be so unhappy and lonely. I'm not looking for love. Not yet, anyway. It's too soon, but I am looking for a woman who is kind enough to care for my kinner. My little Alice—Allie—needs a mudder real bad. And your buwe? Do you think they'd do better with a man in the house?"

She nodded as she looked down at the table cloth. Several crumbs from breakfast were next to her mug and she pushed them together and formed a tiny lump. "They don't listen to me. I don't know if they'd listen to anyone, but sometimes I feel frustrated by my failings as a mudder."

"You're not failing them, Anna. I know you love them and try your hardest. Kinner need parents. Both a mudder and a daed. Maybe we can marry and try to meld our families together. We must think about the possibility. You're the first woman I've met who I think I could care about. I mean really care. Like someday…"

She smiled faintly though tears were merely a shadow away. "Perhaps it could work out. You haven't met my kinner yet though, and I haven't spent time with you or your family."

"I know it's too soon to make a decision. I just want you to know what's going through my mind. I don't want you to think I'm courting you like a man who's never married. It's very different now."

"Jah. I know. For me, too. Jeremiah and I never had eyes for anyone else." Her tears no longer stayed hidden and she lowered her head as she felt them trickle down her cheeks. Then she felt Abe's hand on her arm and he squeezed it gently.

"I would be slow about coming to you as a husband, Anna. It would not happen unless you wanted it to."

She looked up and nodded through her tears. "Jah. I understand what you're saying. I appreciate hearing that. I don't think I could…not now. Maybe not ever."

"I'd accept that."

The back door opened and in came his sister, Naomi, carrying her daughter Becky in one arm and holding his daughter, Allie, with her other hand. "It's cold out there today. Hi, Anna."

"Hullo, Naomi."

The conversation turned to the weather as Abe rose and gathered his daughter in his arms. Allie put her arms around her father's neck as she peeked over at this new woman in their home. Anna patted her arm and said hullo and then tried to engage her in conversation. Instead of responding, Allie burrowed her head in her father's shoulder and avoided eye contact. The boys came into the kitchen and hugged their aunt after she sat her toddler on the floor. Allie pushed away from her father and begged to get on the floor with her cousin, Becky. The two of them had their dolls with them and began playing together.

"Did you have enough venison for your stew?" Naomi asked her brother.

"Plenty. Enough for another meal, unless our guest

eats like a man," he said, winking over at Anna, who shook her head.

"Nee, I'm a small eater."

"That's how you stay so slender," Naomi said as she took off her shawl to hang. "I've put on five pounds since the baby."

"You look gut, schwester. You were too skinny. I was afraid a strong wind would blow you away," he added as he sat back down and watched the little ones playing. "So, Allie, do you want to stay overnight tonight?"

She scowled and shook her head. "Aenti needs me."

"See?" he asked, looking over at Anna, totally frustrated. "It's one excuse after another."

Anna nodded. "It's hard at her age." She knelt down and patted Allie's doll on the head. "How is Katie today?" she asked.

"It's Nancy. Katie stayed home. She was sick to her tummy."

"I'm sorry to hear that. Are they twins?"

Allie nodded, but didn't look up. "I think so."

"Well, they do look alike."

"But Katie sleeps more than Nancy. She's always tired. She misses her mamm."

"Oh, I see." Anna glanced up at Abe and Naomi who were listening intently to their exchange.

"Maybe she'll get a new mamm," Naomi said softly.

"Nee, she only likes the old one," Allie said matter-of-factly.

Naomi let out a sigh. "I left the other kinner with William. He was going to do paper work today, so he said he'd take care of them." She turned to Anna. "I think you met my husband yesterday."

"I met so many people, I'm afraid I don't remember names."

"As long as you remember my name," Abe said with a cute lopsided grin.

Anna felt a blush rise from her neck. It felt like a flirt, and she felt like a teenager.

Chapter Three

Josiah closed his shop later than normal and retreated to the back room which served as a kitchen and dining area—which he never used, and his living room. It was still, even foreboding. He'd been too unwilling to listen to Beth, allowing his anger to take over. Not something he was proud about. It was very unlike him to show such belligerence, and he knelt in prayer to ask for forgiveness.

"Lord, I don't know what got into me. Please forgive my anger and take it from me. I'm sorry I made Beth cry. It was the last thing in the world I wanted to do. Please bless her and bring a man into her life who is gut. Not like me. Just protect her from that English fellow who is not to be trusted. Gott, help me with my business so I can be generous with those less fortunate. I don't need much for myself."

He stopped and wiped his eyes with his sleeve. He never cried. It was necessary to get ahold of himself. This would never do. But he cared so much for her.

Was there anything left for him to do to gain her trust again? He shook his head and returned his attention to the Lord.

"I'm real ashamed of myself, Gott. I need you to make me kinder and a better person. I want to be more like you. Help me accept the single life so I can concentrate on others more. I've been thinking too much about myself. I know that's not right. And if you would, let me feel some peace soon. I hate the way I feel right now. So sad and miserable."

He stopped verbalizing and rested his head against the seat of the wooden chair. He stayed kneeling for several more minutes before rising. His stomach growled and reminded him that he hadn't eaten since early morning. Even when the heart is broken, the body continues its demands.

As he reached for a half loaf of bread from his small counter, he wondered what was in the cupboard. The sliced cheese and liverwurst were gone. Of course, there was always peanut butter. As he reached in the silverware drawer for a knife, he heard a loud knocking on the front door. Maybe he'd just let the person leave. After all, it was obvious he was closed.

After more persistent knocking, he walked up front and looked out the picture window. It was Beth's father. What on earth was he there for? When he opened the door, Isaiah Miller stepped across the threshold. "Sorry to bother you, Josiah, but we're concerned about Beth. She ain't home yet. It's not like her to be so late."

"She left a couple hours ago."

"Did she say if she had errands to run?" Isaiah asked, nervously wrapping his hands around his hat brim which he held in front of him.

"Nee." Josiah wasn't prepared for this. What could have happened? He had to tell her father about her quitting her job. "She didn't leave on gut terms, I'm afraid. In fact, she quit her job."

"Really? My goodness, I thought she was smitten with you, Josiah. What on earth happened?"

"It would be too much to explain and I don't know how she'd feel about my talking about it. I'm concerned, though. Did you check at any of her friend's houses?"

"Nee. Maybe I'll head over to Lydia Cook's place. She's probably her closest friend."

"Do you want me to go with you?"

"Nee, stay here in case she comes back. I still don't understand…"

"Are you still staying at Anna's place while she's away?"

"Jah, I forgot to check at our own house first. Why didn't I think of that? Maybe she had a headache and went straight home."

"I can go over and check if you want," Josiah offered.

"Nee. It's on the way to the Cook's. Sorry to bother you. I'm sure she's okay."

"Do you mind if I come by later to check on things? I still care about your dochder."

Isaiah nodded. "Well, I'm pretty sure she still has feelings for you, too. I heard she gave you the gloves she'd knitted for me. That's a clue right there, don't you think?" He gave Josiah a half-hearted grin and chuckled as he headed for his buggy. "Stop by any time."

Josiah watched as the buggy left the parking lot. What if she'd been in an accident? She sure took off in a hurry. That poor horse hadn't moved that quickly in years, most likely. What if a wheel came off and she ended up in a ditch, or worse yet—was kidnapped! Maybe that English guy had run after her and—

"Stop it!" he said aloud. "Enough doomsday thoughts." He reached for his jacket and headed for the barn to hook up his horse to the buggy. He'd wait a few minutes before riding over to Anna's, just in case Beth showed up at his place.

Abe's boys hung out in the kitchen as Anna rolled the dough for the apple dumplings. Naomi had returned to her home mid-afternoon after a pleasant visit. Allie started to fuss when Abe suggested she stay, so rather than have a scene, he hugged her and allowed her to go back with his sister.

"Mamm made the dough thicker," Benny said, scrunching his brows together.

"It doesn't matter," John reprimanded. "It's gut either way."

"Can I cut up the apples?" Benny asked.

"They don't really get cut up into slices. We have to peel them and core them though. Have you ever used a sharp knife, Ben?" Anna asked.

He nodded, but his brother put his hands on his hips. "Not real sharp. Just a butter knife, Benny. That's not the same."

"Well, I could do it. I know it."

"You'd better ask Daed first," John said as he leaned on the table to watch the process.

"What you can do, is find the cinnamon and sugar for me, Ben," Anna suggested. "That would be a big help."

Ben jumped off the chair and ran to the supply closet where he reached for the cinnamon. The sugar bowl sat next to it, but it came tumbling off the shelf as he accidentally bumped it with his hand. It spilled all over the floor.

"Uh, oh." Ben looked sheepishly over at Anna, who bit her lip.

"Accidents happen. Don't you worry. Just get a dust pan and broom and we'll redd it up lickety-split."

"You're not mad?"

Anna patted his head. "I've done the same thing myself. Sometimes we hurry too much. And the hurried-er we get, the more chance of accidents."

John laughed at his brother's look as he went for the broom. "You look like you've seen a ghost," he teased.

Abe came into the kitchen from the front room where he was adding wood to the fireplace. "What's going on? I thought I heard something crash." He spotted the mess and shook his head. "I've told you to be careful, buwe. Now look at the extra work you've made." He glanced over at Anna who reached for the broom and began sweeping the sugar into a pile.

"It's okay, Abe. We've all made mistakes. Ben's real sorry, aren't you?"

"Jah, that's for sure. She wasn't mad, Daed. Honest."

Anna smiled. "It's just going to take a little longer now. Maybe we can use brown sugar instead."

"I know where that is," John said as he returned to the cupboard. "It's in a box. It can't break."

"Can I help with the apples?" Abe asked Anna as things returned to normal.

"If you'd like to," she answered, pointing to the

washed apples on the drain board. "You can peel them for me and cut away the core."

"All of them?" he asked, glancing over at the dozen apples still dripping wet.

"I thought you'd like extra for your schwester's family."

"Nice idea. Sure." He scrubbed his hands and wiped them dry on a clean towel. Then he began his chore. Anna glanced over and held back a smile. He obviously had never peeled an apple before. He was taking a good half inch of fruit along with the skin. It amused her that he was even trying.

"Am I doing this right?" He asked, looking over at her as she cut the dough into squares.

"Just fine," she answered.

"Hey Daed, those apples look pretty skimpy when you're done taking off the peel. I bet we could make applesauce with your left-overs."

Anna saw Abe's neck turn red. "Well, I'm not real gut at cooking stuff."

Benny giggled and Anna let out a chuckle. "It's gut to try, Abe. That's how we learn."

"I'm better at plowing, I guess," he said, smiling back.

After the apples baked, she left them on top of the griddle in the center of the stove to cool. The aroma was mouth-watering good.

The stew sat on the back of the coal stove simmering away. Abe had added whole carrots and Anna had cut up potatoes. The boys seemed fascinated by everything that transpired. Anna knew it was the fact she was there. A woman in a home makes a difference, she thought as she added seasoning to the venison stew. Abe stood and watched and then suggested they take a walk so he could show her around the farm. It was mild for winter and her shawl gave her enough protection from the occasional breeze. Abe had on a woolen jacket. The boys wanted to follow, but he reminded them of their undone chores. They fussed briefly and then headed for the wood pile where they began collecting firewood for the kitchen.

Anna was impressed with the neatness of the yard. There was still a thin layer of snow left on the ground. When they arrived at the barn, Abe held the wide door open for her and she entered. He then lit a kerosene lamp and placed it on a hook near the stalls. The cows would need milking soon, she noted. They discussed the milking schedules and other details of dairy farming. Then they sat on a couple of bales of hay and made light talk.

Abe became quieter and then asked if she liked his children.

"Oh, jah, they're adorable. And well-behaved."

"For the most part," he said, smiling broadly. "I think they sure like you. They seemed happier than I've seen them for a long while. Denki, Anna."

"Don't thank me. I've thoroughly enjoyed being here. I guess I feel kind of needed."

"Do you think I should come to Pennsylvania soon to meet your family?"

"That would be nice."

"When can I come?"

"Well, whenever you'd like," she said as her heart beat faster. Things were moving quickly. But why not? If they were to become one family, why put it off?

The children's needs were many. Now might be the right time.

"How about next week-end? I can get my *schwoger* to take over my milking while I'm gone."

"Nice having gut in-laws," Anna remarked. "Would you want the kinner to come with you?"

"I think it would be a gut idea. After all, if the kinner don't get along with each other…well—"

"Jah," she said unable to hide her disappointment, "Then what would be the point of us…"

He nodded, looking down at his feet. "The kinner have to come first."

"Jah, they do." Why did he suddenly look the way she felt? Sad and all. "You'll have to get a driver lined up."

"I have a couple people I use. That shouldn't be a problem. Do you have a phone near your home so we can firm things up?"

"A neighbor has a phone shanty by his barn. He's real nice about letting people use it. I have his number memorized."

"Before you leave, I'll write it down and we can plan a time to talk."

"Abe, I have to warn you again about my buwe."

"I think I know what you're saying. Without their daed, they have become a bit difficult and rambunctious. Right? Isn't that what you said?"

She nodded. "They may not be happy having someone new tell them what to do."

"That's understandable, but they'd have to accept the fact that I was now going to be the head of the household. You think they'd be okay with that?"

She shook her head. "I don't honestly know. Sometimes they talk about me re-marrying, but it's never been a real possibility before."

"Anna," he put his hands out and she took hold of them. "All we can do is try. We can pray about it and do our best to help our kinner adjust to a new life. If it's too difficult, we'll remain friends, anyway."

"Jah, I hope so, though we live far apart."

"But you'll want to visit Dinah and Hosea, won't you?"

"I would, but it's not easy to get away. My parents were just kind enough to offer. They've seen how miserable I've been and thought it would be gut for me to have a vacation from the kinner. From my whole life, I guess you can say."

"I'm so glad you're here. Anna, I still believe it's Gott's will that you came. I want for us to try real hard to make this thing work. How about you?"

"Jah, I believe it could be an answer to prayer. Many prayers. You can't believe how many people have prayed for me to find a kind Amish man to marry."

"I hope I'm kind enough for their prayers to be answered. I guess we'd better go check the stew."

They rose and he put his hand under her elbow as he led her towards the entrance. It felt all right. Then he dropped his hand as they walked across the yard to the house. The boys were still lugging in wood. They grinned at Anna and she felt a warmth go through her that seemed to be a special message from above. Gott was gut.

Chapter Four

Beth curled up on her own bed. Strange, but there were no tears. She was grieving for what might have been, yet her eyes were dry as well as her heart. Things worked better in her life when she accepted the single life and didn't concern herself with men. It was her fate. As soon as a man was interested, she'd destroy any chances of a lasting relationship. She was an expert at messing up. What a talent.

She rolled over and glanced at her bedside clock. It was already getting dark out and she realized her parents would be concerned that she had not arrived back at Anna's. Had she really been lying here over two hours? It didn't seem possible. Slowly, she put her feet over the edge of the bed and sat with her head in her hands. She should pray, but no words came. What would she pray anyway?

There was no point in asking Josiah to stop over. His anger had alarmed her. It was a side she'd never seen and she didn't like it. Nee, not one bit. He certainly could have been more gracious about her leaving. Why did he want her there in the first place? They barely spoke since the incident of the gloves. Surely, she wasn't that great a worker. He could find someone in no time to take her place.

The lamp by her bed was out of kerosene thus she made her way carefully down the stairs by holding onto the railing. All of a sudden she heard the front door open. Could it be a robber? She remained motionless until she heard her father's voice calling out her name.

"Jah, I'm here, Daed. No need to shout."

Her father watched as she started down the stairs.

"Good grief, Beth. You had your mudder and me all worked up. Why are you here? You know we're staying at Anna's."

"I'm sorry, Daed. I didn't realize how late it was." She reached the foot of the stairs. Her father lit a lamp and the amber light bounced across his features. His lips were drawn tightly closed. She knew she'd upset him and felt remorse at her thoughtfulness. Just one more thing to dislike about herself. Jah, self-centered, too. Was there any hope?

"Come along then. We don't want to let your mudder worry any longer than she has."

As she followed behind her father in her own buggy, she mulled over her last words with Josiah. He said he thought he'd met the woman of his dreams. Jah, that was funny. Turned out she was the woman of his nightmares! Poor Josiah. Why did she pay any attention to Randy? Vanity. Jah, on top of being self-centered, she was vain and…and…*stupid!* Goodness! All this and no job now. Maybe she could find work at the market in the spring. Some of the older Amish hired younger, stronger girls to help at the stands. It was not even New Year's yet, and it would be a long, long winter.

When they arrived, her mother met them at the door. Anna's children had been fed, but her parents had waited to eat with Beth. Her mother motioned to the table and Beth sat down, nervously turning her napkin in her lap. As Beth explained about leaving her job and being upset, her parents remained silent. The meal was consumed without conversation. Even the children knew things weren't right and remained well-behaved as they played with their Legos in the living room. When they were finished eating, Beth rose to clear the table. "I'll put everything away, Mamm. You go relax."

Rose nodded. Her lips remained turned down. "I need to start getting the kinner settled down for the night." She left Beth in the kitchen alone to her work and her thoughts. She washed the dishes, dried them, and put them all away. As she removed her outer apron, she thought she heard the clopping of horse's hooves on the gravel driveway. Looking out, she saw the lights of a buggy as it headed towards the house. Who would be stopping by so late? She watched as a man climbed down and headed in the direction of the front door. She knew the step and his silhouette. It was Josiah Yoder.

At Abe's, the evening meal was over with quickly. The boys gabbed happily about school and their pet dog and his antics when he was a pup. Anna was amused at their tales and exuberance. She and Abe exchanged glances frequently, sharing the pleasure of their youthful laughter—the first Abe had heard emanating from his children since his Mary had passed away. Oh, how he missed her.

He swallowed the last of his water and leaned back in his chair after excusing the boys who rinsed off their plates and stacked them in the sink. Anna began to rise, but Abe held up his hand. "I'll do it after you leave, Anna. Let's just enjoy our short time together."

She settled back in her chair and smiled over. "Your buwe are so much fun. They're real schmaert."

"Took after their mudder."

"Maybe, but their daed is pretty schmaert, too," she said, smiling broadly.

"Denki for all you've done today. And tomorrow? You'll come early?"

"Probably about the same time. I promised Dinah I'd help her scrub the floors in the morning. Hosea tries, but Dinah says they're sticky sometimes when he's done."

Abe laughed. "I'm afraid we men don't want to become too gut at things like that. Might be called upon too often."

"Oh, jah. That's for certain. I hope Allie will stay with us tomorrow. I want to get to know her better. She's so cute."

"That she is, but stubborn, too."

"From your wife?" she asked, cocking her head as she grinned.

"Nee, I'll take that one."

"I know it must have been difficult for the poor little one to lose not only her mamm, but her bruders and schwester at the same time."

He nodded. "It's only through Gott that we made it this far. And your kind prayers, Anna. You're a fine woman."

"You hardly know me."

"I know enough to know that it would be an honor if one day you'd become my wife."

"And it would be enough not to love the woman you marry?"

"I don't know how to answer that." He looked down, studying a salt shaker while he turned it around in his hands. "I don't know if the gut Lord gives you more than one woman to love in a lifetime. I would like to love someone again someday, and if we marry, I hope it would happen. For both of us. But you know it's the kinner that are the most important."

"Jah. That's exactly how I feel. I'd have to respect and like the man I'd marry, and so far I feel that way about you, but we don't really know each other yet. I'm sure we're both putting out the best side we have."

He laughed. "You too? Jah, I'm trying real hard to look like Mr. Wonderful. I'm hiding my faults from you, Anna. Are you scared?"

"Oh, mercy. You too?" She gave her scariest face and held up her hands like claws.

Benny came in just at that moment and stopped short. "Wow! You look real mean," he said.

Anna dropped her hands to cover her face as she laughed so hard, tears formed. John came running in from the living room and joined in their laughter, though he wasn't quite sure what was so funny. It didn't matter. There was joy in their home. That's what truly mattered. Gott had brought this pretty woman into their lives for a purpose. And John thought he knew what it was.

The next morning after washing down the floors for Dinah, Anna bathed and changed into a fresh dress before waiting for Abe to pick her up. They had decided on one-thirty.

Promptly at half past one, his buggy appeared on the drive.

"See? He's fanatical about promptness," Dinah said as she peeked out the window. "Mary used to complain. She was always a pokey one. It used to drive him crazy. Mary just laughed at him."

"Jah."

Dinah looked over at her friend. "I'm sorry, I shouldn't talk so much about Mary."

"But she was your friend. Of course you should. It may help me to know more about her. I don't have any expectation of taking her place—even if we marry. And Abe won't take the place of Jeremiah, but I feel pleasure when I'm with him and his buwe. Like there's purpose."

Dinah nodded. "We'll talk later. You'd better get your shawl. He's coming up the walk now."

After leaving the house, Abe held his hand out for her as she climbed into the buggy. It was sweet and thoughtful of him. She appreciated his good manners. They were more relaxed today as they drove together. Allie was already at the house with his sister, Naomi, who would not be staying long since her other children needed her. She had brought Becky with her since she was the youngest.

When they came in through the kitchen door, Abe knelt down and motioned for Allie to come over and hug him. She walked over and received her hug and then looked up at Anna, expectantly. Anna knelt down and extended her arms. Slowly, the child walked over and accepted the invitation. As the chubby little arms surrounded Anna's neck, she could feel tears forming. She looked up at Abe who was standing now in front of her. His eyes were glazed over as well. Not a word was spoken. When Allie broke the embrace, she ran into the other room where the boys were playing. Anna stood and Naomi reached for one of her hands. "Denki."

It was a special moment. Abe knew at that moment he wanted this to work out. All that was left was a visit on his part to meet Anna's family.

Chapter Five

Beth's father greeted Josiah with a single shake of the hand as was their custom. Rose came down after putting the children to bed and stood in the background with Beth.

Josiah looked relieved as he caught sight of Beth and allowed a slight smile as he nodded towards her. She did not reciprocate.

"As you can see, our prodigal dochder has returned."

"Where was she?"

Beth wondered if she was invisible the way they talked about her as if she wasn't even present. Even that annoyed her.

"I can speak for myself," she announced moving forward to stand beside her father. "I wanted to be in my own room for a while."

Josiah looked down at his feet and nodded. "I understand."

No one spoke for several moments. Then her father invited him to join them in the living room. Anna was surprised he accepted. She made excuses to return to the kitchen.

"Maybe Josiah would like some tea, Beth."

"I doubt it. He's a coffee drinker," she said as she made her way through the living room to the kitchen.

"Then put the coffee pot on," her father called after her.

"Nee, denki for asking, but I must get back home. I just wanted to be sure she was safe."

Beth turned at the threshold of the kitchen and stared at him. "Why should you care?"

"Of course he cares, Beth. After all, you work for him."

"Not anymore."

"I really must go," Josiah said, turning towards the door.

Rose hadn't said a single word. It was extremely awkward for everyone.

"Well, don't be a stranger," Isaiah said half-heartedly as he followed him to the door. After Josiah's quick retreat, Isaiah closed the door and turned toward his daughter. "That was inexcusable, Beth. How could you be so rude to our guest?"

"You wouldn't understand. You think he's such a fine gentleman, but you didn't see the way he treated me earlier. He was totally rude and out of hand. He doesn't care about me. He just wanted to make a gut appearance now."

Rose spoke for the first time. "He certainly fooled me. He looked scared to death until he spotted you. That's not a man who doesn't care. I don't know what happened at his shop, but I'd be willing to bet you pushed the poor man to his limits."

"Oh, it's always my fault!"

"Beth, I think you should go to you and Rachel's room," her father said sternly. "You're getting out of hand—with everyone."

"Maybe it's your time of month," her mother said under her breath.

"OOOooo," Beth uttered loudly as she stomped up the stairs to her niece's room. Hopefully, she'd be asleep by now.

The way she felt was certainly not befitting of an Amish woman. Nee, she certainly wasn't the modest, quiet, soft-spoken woman she was raised to be. Poor Mamm. She tried so hard. At least she had produced Anna, who was a dream Amish girl. Everything Beth was not.

Beth looked over at her little niece, who appeared to be sound asleep already. Then she tiptoed to the front window and looked towards the road. Goodness, Josiah's buggy was still sitting at the edge of their property. Why on earth wasn't he gone by now? Then she watched as he slowly made the turn towards his home. A wave of sorrow ran through her. It was as if she was watching happiness moving away from her forever. It felt like she was at a turning point. All possibilities of a normal Amish life as wife and mother were now cut off and she stood empty and barren unable to change the course of events. Perhaps it was time to think about the world outside. Was it too late to go for an education? Too late to try for a totally new life?

She reached over to remove her leather shoes and then collapsed on her bed. The only physical sensation she felt was her heart beating rapidly against her chest. Did it create a sound or was she merely aware of the change taking place inside her as she allowed her emotions to surface? Her doubts and conflicting thoughts caused further anxiety. Had she been too hard on Josiah? Did he still care? Or was all this confusion just a result of her inability to accept the fact that she really did love Josiah Yoder? And now he was gone. She turned her head, pressed it against the pillow and allowed the tears to flow silently.

Josiah was relieved to know Beth was safe in her home. When he first saw her standing behind her father he wanted to run over and grab her, beg for forgiveness, and carry her away in his arms. Instead he had foolishly talked as if she was non-existent. What did she think of him now? Wasn't it enough that he'd raised his voice to her and behaved like an immature teenager? Maybe if he'd just sat down and discussed the whole Christmas gift thing, they could have cleared the air and resumed their relationship. But how could he go back to being second choice? Or worse yet—last choice. Maybe she was merely feeling the pressure of her age when she showed interest in him to begin with. After all, most Amish girls were married by the time they were twenty-four.

After taking care of the horse, he went into his empty shop. He lit a couple of lamps and looked around at all the inventory he had accumulated in such a short time. It had been exciting to start his business, especially having Beth nearby helping him. But now, he felt like a deflated balloon tossed in the trash. It was gut that things were slow during the holidays. He hoped his enthusiasm would return and he'd fill his orders in a timely fashion. At the moment, nothing excited him.

What he had felt for Christina years back was nothing to his emotions for Beth. What was so special about the woman anyway? She certainly was opinionated. And quick to anger. Not very gut qualities for an Amish woman. Yet, it was her difference that he found so attractive. She was her own person. She did have a case of 'foot in mouth' disease, but he found her fascinating in spite of it. Or was it because of it.

Goodness. What a confusing night it had been.

He retreated to his small kitchen and looked for something to eat. Finally, he spread raspberry jam on a piece of stale bread he found in a drawer. Someone had brought the jam over for him when he opened his shop. He couldn't even remember who it had been. No matter. There was half a quart of milk left in the refrigerator. After pouring himself a glass, he sat on one of his mismatched wooden kitchen chairs and looked around. What did he have to offer a woman at this stage? Yah, the business was growing—quickly—but this was his home right now and it was pretty pathetic even in his eyes. He didn't even keep it neat. Of course Beth wasn't really interested in pursuing a relationship with him. Yet he remembered their kiss. The sweet, tender, loving kiss. She surely hadn't faked her feelings. Had she?

He pulled the crust off the top of the bread and chewed it slowly before washing it down with the milk. Not only had he lost Beth as a friend, but he lost an excellent worker as well. He couldn't very well get Lydia Cook back. She was the head teacher now and last he heard, she was thoroughly enjoying it. Maybe he'd put out feelers at church. Maybe he'd find an older woman who wanted to make a little extra pocket money. It would be safer. Jah, that was a gut idea. Maybe an old widow. She'd have to be quick minded. Clever with customers. Intelligent. In other words, just like Beth— only safe. Someone he would not become attached to in a personal way. A motherly figure would be nice. Even a grand-motherly figure.

Josiah placed the soiled plate on top of several others in the sink. Tomorrow he'd clean up. Tomorrow. Then Sunday he'd see Beth at the church service. Maybe he'd try to talk to her. Just a little. Nothing serious. Then again, maybe he'd avoid her. Time would tell. Right now he just hoped he could get his mind on something else. Why did her laughter keep haunting him?

As he passed through the door to his workshop with his kero lantern in hand, he stopped and looked at a television cabinet he was working on. It needed another finish coat. He set the lantern down and lit two others. Then he reached for the can of finish and went to work. That was his answer. Work.

Anna spent a restless night at her friend's house. During the night, she removed the photo from her suitcase. It had been taken when she and Jeremiah were married. Taken in secret by an English friend with her phone camera and later printed off. It was the only picture she had of her deceased husband, and she treasured it. For the first time, it gave her little pleasure. In fact, it brought on a wave of fresh sorrow.

Perhaps she should cancel her plans to visit with Abe again. It was probably too soon to think about re-marrying. When she was wed, she thought she and her husband would live long lives and grow old together, living in the same house with their children and grandchildren surrounding them. But it was not to be. At thirty-five, in the prime of life, a serious heart attack took him home to be with his heavenly Father. The months that followed were the most difficult of Anna's life.

Why was she here? Had it been God who brought her attention to Abe's tragic situation? She'd cut the article out and placed it on her refrigerator to pray for him and his remaining children. It was odd when she thought about it. There were other tragedies that did not receive her consideration, yet for some reason her heart was deeply affected by Abe Stoltzfus and his young family. And now they had been brought together. Abe was sure it was the Lord at work and she quite frankly, couldn't argue with his conclusion. It was just too strange to be a coincidence. Besides, that was how God worked sometimes.

She put the photo back in her suitcase and tucked her pillow under her neck. It was nearly dawn and she'd only had about four hours sleep. It was time to pray and pray with fervor. She spent half an hour sharing her concerns and desires with God and then slept peaceably until eight in the morning, late for an Amish person.

Five minutes before one, Anna made her way through three inches of new-fallen snow to the edge of the driveway. Abe grinned at her as he pulled in a minute later. As he helped her in, he told her how much he appreciated her promptness.

"I've always been on time for things," she said. "My mamm drilled it into us."

"It shows consideration for others," he said, nodding. "The kinner are excited about their big day today. I can't tell you how much it means to all of us to have you come and bake cakes for their birthdays and make it a real celebration."

"I'm excited myself. I love parties. Is your sister coming?"

"Jah, she'll be there along with all the kinner. Her husband, William, will be there too. We got word to our whole family. Even my parents are coming. It's hard for them because of my grossmammi's Altzheimer's. They wanted to bring her along, but she has a bad cold and will stay with a cousin."

"And your brother and sister who live with them?"

"Jah, Sam will come and Eve wouldn't miss it."

"You said she has Down syndrome?"

"Jah, but she's pretty gut. Eve's a sweetheart. Everyone loves her."

"You have twin brothers too, don't you?"

"Jah, but they live too far away. You'll meet them if…"

She nodded. She knew he was thinking of their possible wedding, but just couldn't quite get the words out. Just as well. It might never happen.

"I'd better make a third cake," she said, smiling over.

"Two will be fine. Everyone will bring a dish for supper, we always get piles of cookies."

"Jah, I never worry about having food enough with Amish folk. We might not have riches, but we always eat well," she added.

When they arrived, there were two other buggies parked in the back.

"I guess my family is starting to show up. We weren't planning on a party this year, but I think it's important to keep things as normal as possible for the kinner. You inspired it. I'm very grateful," Abe said as he reached for her hand. They headed towards the house.

The boys ran over to greet them when they came in the back door. Naomi was wiping down counters from their noon meal when they arrived, but she stopped to give Anna a warm hug. "Even Allie was excited when I told her about the party," she said, reaching for Anna's shawl.

"Goodness, it's gotten cold out there," Anna said as she handed over her shawl. "Where is Allie?"

"She's playing in the front room with my kinner. Want me to get her?"

"Nee, I'll go say hullo to everyone." Abe followed her in and Allie came right over. She went to her father first and then automatically reached for Anna, who knelt down to hug her.

"You making cakes?"

"Jah. Birthday cakes for your bruders."

"Do I get a cake all to myself?"

Anna laughed. "No, little one. We are all sharing."

"You come back for my birthday and make me my very own cake?" she asked with huge chocolate eyes.

"And when is your birthday?"

Allie shrugged and ran off, calling back as she went. "Better ask daed. He knows."

Anna turned to Abe, who was grinning like the Cheshire cat. "She's quite a character," he said, shaking his head.

"Jah, she's a doll. I bet my Rachel will love her. She always wanted a schwester."

Abe touched Anna's cheek with one finger. "Maybe we can make that happen."

"I'd better start the cakes, Abe. As more people start arriving, it will get harder to work in your kitchen."

"I laid out all the things you told me too, including the chocolate. Naomi will lend a hand. She knows where everything is. Like pans and things."

"Gut. You go relax with your kinner and we'll have the cakes in the oven quick as a wink."

"I believe that," he said as he stepped in the next room to talk to his brother-in-law William.

Naomi was bubbling away about the family as she helped whip up one of the batters. Anna and she worked well together and stayed off serious topics, just enjoying the day. Abe's boys ran in every few minutes to check on the progress of the cakes, though they would not be allowed to see them once they were frosted.

Allie pulled on Anna's skirt several times to get a lick from the wooden spoon Anna used to prepare the frostings, and then ran back to play.

"She needs a mamm so bad," Naomi said once.

Anna didn't respond except to smile over. Things were certainly moving quickly. In the back of her mind, she feared Abe's meeting with her boys. His children were so well-behaved in comparison. It could put an end to any further discussion of marriage and she had already decided she would probably accept a proposal if one was forthcoming. He was a kind man and she approved of his parenting skills. His boys adored him, though he was strict when he had to be. She'd already observed his tone of voice when they started to get out of line. Though he never really raised his voice, the inflection he used told them exactly when they had gotten to the edge of his patience. Precisely what her own boys needed. *Oh, Lord, please let this work out.*

The cakes were iced and set in the pantry out of sight when Abe's parents arrived with Sam and Eve. They were introduced to Anna and then they went in the front room to join the others. Anna was slightly nervous. His mother had seemed cool when they met, but Naomi said that was just the way their mother presented herself. She assured Anna the whole family was hoping for Abe to re-marry—for the sake of the children.

Abe's father looked like both of his sons. Sam, who was thirty, was taller and slightly thinner than Abe. Though Abe had kept his beard, his brother, being single, was still clean shaven. He was an outgoing man, even grabbed Naomi and swung her around before kissing her on the cheek. He shook Anna's hand and then held it for an extra moment. He looked into her eyes before commenting. "You look like a nice Amish lady. If my bruder doesn't have any ideas, let me know."

Naomi giggled and swatted him on the arm. "You've managed to stay single so far, Sam. Better not trespass here."

"Nee. I'm kidding." Then his smile turned down and he leaned closer to Anna. "My bruder is a gut man, Anna, but he needs a woman. I fear for him sometimes. He's too sad. I hope you can make him smile again."

"I think I'd like to try, Sam. I agree, he is a very nice man."

Sam seemed pleased with her answer and leaned over to kiss her on her cheek. "Invite me to your wedding, *bitte*."

She nodded as she smiled back. Though Abe was too far to hear what was discussed, he grinned and nodded at Anna.

Eve was in charge of the balloons. She and the older cousins blew up over three dozen and tied them with colorful ribbons before hanging them from the ceiling. She was in her glory and never stopped smiling. Anna sensed Eve accepted her since every time they passed each other, Eve patted her on the shoulder and smiled broadly.

When it was time for dessert, Abe and Naomi carried in the cakes with the candles ablaze. Everyone sang, first to John, who would turn eleven in less than a week, and then to Benny, who had a month to wait—but couldn't. They always shared their birthdays, according to Naomi, who said it saved her parents the long drive back a month later.

After everyone had left, including Naomi and her family, Abe put the boys down early. They didn't fuss since neither had slept well the night before anticipating their party. Allie had hesitated when Abe asked if she'd like to stay for the night, but she ended up going home with her aunt at the last minute.

Anna fluffed up the cushions on the sofa and plopped down.

Abe sat next to her and took her hand in his. "Tired?"

"Exhausted. I guess I haven't slept too well since I've been here."

"The bed too hard?"

"Nee, it's probably all the excitement."

"Jah, I know what you mean. I've had some problems sleeping myself. Well, Anna Miller, what do you think about my crazy family?"

She laughed and tilted her head. "I love them. Everyone is so friendly. The only person who I didn't get to meet was that woman who came in before we served the cake and left off packages for the boys. Was that one of your relatives?"

Abe's smile dropped. "I'm sorry, I should have introduced you. That was Mary's mamm."

"Oh. The poor lady."

"Jah, it's been rough on her, too. We invited her to come to the party, but she just left off the gifts."

"She didn't want to stay?"

"I'm afraid it was too difficult for her. She asked who you were."

"What did you tell her?"

"The truth."

"That you might be marrying me someday?"

"Jah." He ran his hand through his thick dark hair. "She said it was gut that I'd re-marry, but she didn't want to meet you. Not yet anyway."

"I understand."

"Jah, I do too. She's a fine woman and I know someday if things work out with us, she'll accept you, but…"

"You don't have to explain. I truly understand. I'd probably feel the same way. I hope though, that the kinner will always have a special place in their hearts for Mary's family."

Abe smiled over and squeezed her hand. "You're remarkable, Anna Miller. You are a compassionate lady.

I like you very much and I'm excited to meet your kin-ner. Next week-end should work?"

"I believe it will."

"Then it will be easier for me to say good-bye to you tonight."

"And I believe it's almost time for Hosea to arrive," she said. All she wanted at that moment was a good night's sleep. What a week-end.

"I'm afraid it is," Abe said. "It's almost nine."

A few minutes later, Dinah's husband came in his buggy to pick her up. He stayed a few minutes to talk and then headed out to the buggy while Abe sur-rounded Anna with her shawl. He took her hands in his. "Denki, for everything, Anna. I look forward to next week-end."

Anna was surprised at the pleasure his human touch gave her. He was indeed a fine man. And that was enough. For now.

They walked out to the waiting buggy and she turned to wave as they left his drive and made the turn on the country road. It would be a long week.

Chapter Six

On the way home to Pennsylvania, Anna asked the driver to stop at a gift shop she'd seen on the way over so she could purchase gifts for the children. She was fortunate to find a giraffe for Rachelle and a new softball for her boys. They were good about sharing, especially when it came to sports items. Since it was noon, she sat with the driver as they ate lunch in an indoor mall area. Dinah had prepared egg salad sandwiches for them. They were delicious and she'd even sent along cole slaw in a plastic container. Anna's driver, Ted Darby, ordered coffee for both of them and even brought over ice cream cones from one of the stands in the food court.

They got back on the road and resumed their travel. Ted was a pleasant man, but concentrated on his driving, which suited Anna perfectly. She preferred spending this time thinking over her situation. The idea of re-marrying was not as strange as it had been earlier and she was quite taken with Abe as a potential mate.

He seemed so mannerly and considerate. She was confidant he wouldn't expect her to be intimate—at least for a year or so. If even then.

She couldn't picture herself wearing nightclothes in front of another man. Her wedding night had been difficult in some ways since she was raised to be very modest. Even allowing him to unwind her braid and brush her hair the way he had, had seemed embarrassing at the time. She smiled thinking about Jeremiah. It was so cute the way he had kissed her hair before reaching for her lips. *Oh, Jeremiah, I miss you so.* Tears escaped as she recaptured her early memories of their life together. It was in the past. She kept telling herself she must move on. It was the only sensible thing to do. The boys came to her mind and she nodded. *Jah, if not for myself, then for my buwe and dochder. They need a daed.* She wiped her eyes with her sleeve and sat back to enjoy the snow-covered landscape flashing past. Soon she'd be home and there'd be little time for dwelling on her past.

"Grossmammi, why ain't Mamm home yet?" young Mark wanted to know.

Rose patted his shoulder. "I told you, it's a long trip and the roads may be slippery. She should be here in time for supper. Now go get your toys picked up."

"That's Luke's job."

His grandfather, who had been listening as he perused the Amish paper he was holding, set the paper down on his lap and scowled at his grandson. "Mark, do as your grossmammi told you."

Mark stood a moment contemplating the consequences and then nodded and left the kitchen.

"I hope they listen as well for our dochder as they do for you, Isaiah."

"It helps that I'm a man, I'm thinking." He raised the paper and resumed reading.

Rose walked over to the stove and stirred vegetable soup. "She should be home by now, don't you think?"

"Depends."

"On?"

"Lots of things. The roads, how many stops they made, when they got started. Not to worry, Rose. You always imagine the worst."

"I can't help it. Ever since Jeremiah…"

"Jah, I know. One never knows."

Rachel came scurrying into the kitchen, clutching one of her faceless dolls. "Mark said my dolly is weird. That's mean!"

"Now, now. You know how buwe can be. They say mean things sometimes. Just ignore them."

Isaiah folded his paper and rose from his rocking chair in the corner of the kitchen. "I'd better have a talk with that bu. He's been acting up all day."

"I think he's just excited about Anna coming home," Rose remarked, laying her wooden spoon on a plate. "Come, Rachel, you can help me set the table."

Rachel smiled up at her grandmother. "I can do it all by myself, Mammi. Remember?"

"Oh, I do now that you mention it. You're a gut maed."

"What does *dummkopf* mean, Mammi?" the child asked as she reached in the drawer for the silverware.

"Goodness, why do you ask?"

"Cause Mark said I was that funny word."

"Don't you listen to him, Rachel. Mark uses bad words sometimes."

"Is it a dirty word?"

Rose sighed. "It means 'dummy' in Deitsch, little one. So in a way, I'd say it's a dirty word."

"*He's* the real dummy, right, Mammi?"

Rose laughed out loud. "We don't have any dummies in our family, Rachel. Now let me get the napkins for you."

Rachel straightened out the silverware so they were lined up perfectly. Her petite mouth was drawn down. Finally, she asked, "Mammi, do you think Mamm will come home?"

Rose nearly dropped the soup bowls she was taking down from the cabinet. She rested them on the counter and turned to look at her granddaughter. "Why would you ask that, honey?"

"Because I heard Luke say she was probably gonna look for gut kids and a new man to marry."

"Mercy, that bu thinks of the strangest things. Nee, not to worry. Your mamm is coming home real soon. She's on her way right this minute. If she ever does remarry, she's not going to leave you kinner."

"But Daed left us," the child said softly, her voice wavering.

"Come here, child." Rachel took several steps to reach her grandmother, who knelt and swept her into her arms. "Your poor daed didn't have anything to say about his leaving. You know that. The gut Lord wanted him to come home, is all. Sometimes young people are called home earlier than the old ones. It's just the way it works, but he didn't leave because he wanted to. And as far as your mamm goes, she would never, ever, leave her kinner. She loves you more than anything in the world."

"But she yells a lot. Especially at my bruders. They think she doesn't care much anymore."

"Oh, dear child. She's been through so much. She just doesn't know how to handle everything all by herself."

"But we're here to help."

"You're still all kinner. Your mamm is doing the best she knows how. Maybe someday she'll find a man who would be a gut daed for you all and then things could get back to normal—almost."

"I hope so. I'm tired of my bruders yelling and being mean all the time. At least with you here, Daadi made them be gut. Maybe we should all live with you when Mamm gets home."

"Don't count on it, little one. Most women like having their own home where they make all the decisions."

"Mmm. I bet you're right. She can be *real* bossy."

Rose laughed and stood up. "I think I hear a car pulling in, Rachel. Go look out the front window and see if it's your mamm's driver."

Rachel took off immediately and started yelling. "It is! It's Mamm! She found us again."

Rose smiled as she sent a prayer of thanks for the safe return of her eldest dochder. She called up the stairs to tell Beth about her sister's arrival.

Then she joined the rest of the family as they gathered at the doorway.

Abe set his glass of water aside at supper and sat back in his chair. His boys began to rise to clear the table. "Wait, sohns, let's talk first."

They exchanged glances as they sat back down. "What do you want to talk about, Daed?" asked John.

"Well, first off, how did you like having Anna Miller here with us?"

Benny grinned. "She's real nice. And pretty, too. Don't you think so, Daed?"

His neck flushed red as he cleared his throat. "Jah, she's a nice lady. How about you John? What do you think?"

John took his time before answering. "I guess she's nice. She makes gut cake, I'll say that."

"But?" Abe asked.

"I'm just wondering if she's always so nice. I mean, we don't know her real well. Are you going to marry her or something?" His eyes questioned as well as his lips.

"I'm thinking about it real serious-like," Abe admitted. "But if you buwe don't like her, I wouldn't even consider it."

"I think we like her," Benny said quickly. "At least I do. She smiles a lot."

"So did Mamm," John added quickly.

"But she's dead!" Benny said, his eyes filling.

"Now, let's not get upset," Abe said. "Your bruder just made a statement about your mudder, Benny. And it was true. She did smile a lot." This conversation was getting more difficult with each word. Abe cleared his throat. "We have to accept the fact that your mudder will not be returning. Life goes on. We've all grieved for her—for what might have been, and I'm thinking we need to move on."

"We're doing okay," John added.

"What about your schwester? She doesn't even

live with us anymore. How do you think your mudder would feel about that?"

Benny nodded. "She'd be mad."

"Nee, she would not," John said, staring angrily at his brother.

"She would be unhappy, John," Abe said, resting his one hand on his beard and stroking it thoughtfully. "That's the main reason I'm thinking about asking Anna to marry me. I want my kinner together."

"What if you don't like her?" John asked, his brows knotted.

"But I do like her. She's very nice and kind. She's been through a lot too, you know. Her husband died young, leaving her with four young ones."

"What if they're bad kids?" John continued.

"Well, we're going to find out next week-end. I plan to get a driver and spend time with her and her kinner and I want you both to come with me."

"How old are her kinner?" Benny asked.

"Let's see, I wrote that down." He reached into his pants' pocket and opened up a slip of paper. "Her oldest is a boy. Luke is ten."

"Same as you, John," Benny noted with a smile.

"I'm almost eleven, remember?"

"Oh, I forgot." Benny looked down at his empty plate.

"That's close enough," Abe said, rather sternly. "The next boy is eight. His name is Matthew."

"No way!" Benny became ecstatic again.

"Big deal," John remarked under his breath.

Abe gave John a look which settled him down. "Then Mark is seven and she has a dochder who is five. Her name is Rachel."

"She could take care of Allie," Benny said, grinning.

"Jah, maybe," Abe said with a nod. "According to Anna, she loves boppli and little ones."

"It sounds great, Daed," Benny added. "I think you should marry her and we can be one big happy family again."

John stood up and shoved his chair away from the table. "You're a jerk, Benny! We'll never be a happy family again!"

Before Abe could respond, John ran for the stairs and headed for his bedroom.

Benny's mouth dropped open and he stared over at his father. "I didn't mean to make him mad, Daed."

Abe reached across and patted his son's hand. "It's okay, Benny. John is feeling lots of sadness today. We have to honor his feelings."

"Aren't you going to punish him?"

"Nee. Not this time, Sohn. It's gut he got the words out. He's still grieving."

"So am I, Daed, but I think Mamm would like Anna Miller and want her to help us out."

"Hopefully, your bruder will come around. Maybe once he meets her kinner, he'll change his feelings."

"And if he doesn't, Daed?"

Abe shook his head. "I don't know, Benny. I don't know."

"Well, I'm gonna pray real hard about it, because I'd like a nice lady to tuck me in bed at night. I'm not too big for that kind of stuff. Besides, she smelled real pretty—like the lilacs when they come out."

Abe smiled over at his son. "Jah, she does. I think prayer is the answer, Sohn. In the meantime, let's redd-up the kitchen and play a game of checkers. Hopefully, John will join us soon."

"Are you going to go talk to him?"

"I think he needs to be alone for a while. John will talk when he's ready."

Benny nodded and began clearing the table.

Chapter Seven

Anna hugged everyone as she came through the door. Rachel was last as she hung back while her brothers embraced their mother. Then she accepted a warm hug from Anna and looked over as the driver brought in the suitcase and bag from the gift store. After he was paid, Rachel stood with her hands on her hips. "Did you find a giraffe for me?" she asked.

"Rachel, shame on you," Rose said to her granddaughter. "Your mamm just got in the door."

"Yeah, you're greedy," Mark said, glaring at his sister.

"I'm not! Mamm said she'd get me a giraffe, is all."

"Well, let me get my shawl off and my shoes, and we can check and see what's in the toot."

Anna turned towards her parents as the children went for the bag. "Were they gut for you?"

"Most of the time," her father responded. "They're a handful, though."

"Oh jah. You can say that again," Anna said with half a smile.

"Rachel was real gut," her mother replied. "Helped me a lot."

"Jah, I figured she'd be fine."

The boys started pulling on the bag and it began to rip open. "Buwe, put the toot down and wait for your mother," Isaiah said firmly. They looked over and dropped the bag with a thud.

Anna bent down and took out the giraffe first and handed it to her daughter.

"He's so cute, Mamm. Denki," Rachel said, holding the foot-long stuffed animal to her chest.

"What did you get us?" Matthew asked, trying to peer in the bag.

"Wait. I have something for your grossmammi and daadi." She removed a tin filled with salt-water taffy and handed it over to her mother.

"Oh, I love it! I haven't had any for years."

"I know. You talked about it a few weeks ago."

"I did? I don't even remember. Denki, Anna. That was real nice of you, wasn't it, Isaiah?"

"Oh, jah. Hope I get at least one piece," he said with a grin.

"I want some, too," Mark said as he grabbed it out of his grandmother's hand.

"That's quite enough, Mark," Anna said, her voice raised. "Go upstairs and settle."

"You just got home!"

"And you are being rude and naughty." So nothing had changed. Maybe they'd been good for her parents, but things were back to the new norm. Awful. She almost dreaded the upcoming week-end when Abe would arrive and be introduced to her kinner. What man would put up with her wild family?

"Are you hungry, Anna? We held off supper till you got home," her mother said.

"Wait," Luke said, "Didn't you get me something?"

"Oh, I did. I bought something for all three of you buwe to play with." She reached in the bag and took out the softball and handed it over.

"Denki, Mamm," Luke said as he showed it to Matthew. "Can we go outside and throw it back and forth?"

"It's pretty cold out there," Anna said, as she weighed the cold against the potential peace. "I guess it's okay. Just put on your warm jackets and knit hats first."

They took the ball and headed for their coats and then Anna followed her mother into the kitchen. Her father trailed behind holding Rachel's hand. She gripped her new animal by his neck with her free hand.

"Tell us all about your trip," her mother said as she laid out a plate of salted crackers and a pitcher of milk with several glasses. "Then we'd better have our supper."

"First, where's Beth?"

"Oh, she hasn't come down yet. I think she's still trying to get over a headache."

"I should go say hullo first. If she's better, I want her down here so I don't have to repeat everything."

"Oh, that much to tell," her father said with a wink.

"Jah, lots and lots of news," she said as she made her way up the stairs.

When she got to the room Beth was staying in, she knocked. "Can I come in, Beth?"

"Sure."

When Anna opened the door, she saw it was dimly lit. Her sister was propped up on pillows with a book in her hands. "Mamm said you had a headache."

"Jah, but I'm better now. How was your trip?"

"Gut, but I want you to hear too. Do you feel well enough to join us downstairs?"

Beth tried to smile. It was difficult. "Sure. I'm anxious to hear about Dinah's new boppli. Is she cute?"

"Oh, adorable! You'd love her."

"Where are your kinner? It's awful quiet."

"Well, Mark is being punished and the other buwe are outside playing. I bought them a new softball."

"No wonder it's quiet. I'll come down then. Just give me a minute."

"Take your time. I'll head down, though. I am hungry. Mamm held off supper."

"I smelled soup cooking. I guess I'll have a bowl."

"Let me go check if it's ready. I guess I'll hold off telling everyone about my trip until after we eat."

Beth shook her head and sighed. "It must have been nice to get away," she said to her sister.

"It was wonderful-gut, I have to admit."

After a rather subdued meal due to Isaiah's stern expression, the children became restless.

"Mamm, can I go play with my other stuffed animals? I want them to meet Gerry, my giraffe," Rachel asked.

"Sure, honey. Go on. I'll see you in a few minutes."

Then the boys were permitted to leave the table and they went into the front room to finish a game of Yahtzee. It left the adults alone to talk.

"I've met someone. A man," Anna started.

No one spoke. They just looked at each other in shock.

"Go on," her father said.

"You won't believe who he is! Remember the members of an Amish family who got killed last summer in Ohio?"

"I vaguely remember," her mother said, staring.

"I do," said Beth. "It was a horrible buggy accident. After you told me about it, I prayed for the widower and his kinner for a couple months."

"Well, I met him!"

"Nee!" Her mother put her hand to her heart. "Amazing!"

Anna nodded. "That's what I thought. So did he. He kept saying I was an answer to prayer. We like each other a lot. I spent time with him and his kinner who survived."

"Well, I'll be," Rose finally got out.

Isaiah pulled on his beard and waited for more information.

Beth still looked shocked.

"He wants to come to Pennsylvania and meet my family next week-end."

"Why?" Beth finally asked.

"Because we're talking about getting married."

"Oh my," Rose said softly.

"That sounds like a gut idea," Isaiah said, bobbing his chin up and down. "Jah, your kinner need a full-time man around the house. Rachel, too."

"But do you like him enough to marry him?" Beth asked. "I mean, good grief girl, you just met him."

"I know. It's a little scary, but he's so nice, Beth. I

know you'll like him and everyone's been telling me that's what I need."

"I hope your kinner don't scare him away," Beth said. "They'd scare me away."

"Not *nice*, Schwester! They're not that bad."

"Oh, jah, they are. Admit it."

"Now, let's not paint a worse picture than it is," Rose said, her mouth turned down. "Hopefully, they'll behave better when he visits. Where will he stay? Certainly not here."

"He has cousins in the next district. He's going to see if he can stay there."

"The kinner could stay with us, I guess," Rose said.

"I don't know. He also has a dochder who's nearly four. She's been staying with his schwester and I don't know if she'll be coming with him."

"How many kinner does he have?" Isaiah asked.

"Three. John is turning eleven next week and Benny will be nine in February. They are really nice kinner. Well-behaved."

Rose nodded. "I hope it works out for you, honey, if that's what you want. But don't count on anything yet. You don't want to be disappointed if it doesn't work out."

"I know. I'm nervous about the week-end."

"You should be," Beth said.

"Beth, you're so encouraging," Anna scolded.

"I'm just being realistic. It's all happening too quickly."

Anna let out a long breath. "But it does seem as if God arranged it. It really does. Who ever thought I'd one day meet him and we'd hit it off so well."

"Well, you are pretty to look at," Beth added.

"And very sweet," Rose added.

"And would make a gut mudder for his kids," Isaiah said.

"That's really what this is all about. Our kinner," Anna admitted. "We kinda need each other."

"I hope it would be more than that, Anna," Beth said. "You'd be his wife. You know what that means."

Isaiah looked over and frowned at his younger daughter. "We don't need to get into that discussion. I'm sure your schwester has considered everything."

"I have and I'd rather not talk about that part."

Beth shrugged. "Glad it's not me."

"You'll be married soon enough now that you and Josiah—"

Beth stood up and started for the stairs. "My headache is back, if you'll excuse me." She directed her gaze straight ahead and climbed the steps to the second floor.

Anna looked over at her parents. "What was that all about?"

Rose shrugged. "I have no idea. Maybe she scared him away, too. She quit her job, you know."

"Really? That must have just happened."

"Before you left," Rose said.

"She didn't even mention it."

"Maybe she didn't want to upset you before your trip."

"Oh, golly. I was really hoping this was it."

"We all were," Isaiah added. "Maybe they'll make up."

"It didn't sound that way when I talked to her," Rose said.

"Should I go speak to her?" Anna asked.

"I'd wait till she's ready to talk about it."

Anna nodded. "And here I was all excited about my news. I feel bad now. Maybe she didn't really have a headache at all and just wanted to be alone."

"It's hard to tell with your schwester. She's not an easy person to know. I'm her mamm and sometimes I don't understand her."

Anna leaned back in her chair and folded her arms. "She's even hard on herself. Oh well." She smiled over at her parents. "I so appreciate you watching the kinner for me."

"Looks like Gott may have had a reason to get you to Ohio," Isaiah remarked.

Anna's smile spread across her face. "See? Even you think that."

"I hope it works out for you, Anna," he said. "Just don't raise your hopes too high."

"I'll try not to, but he's the first man I've met who I'd even remotely consider marrying."

"That's a gut sign," her mother said nodding in agreement. "You know you'll probably never feel for another man the way you did for Jeremiah. That's once in a lifetime."

Anna nodded. "I don't expect to, but I could sure use some company in the evenings when the kids go to bed. That's my hardest time. Just someone sitting in the same room with me would help. We don't even have to talk."

"Jah. I understand," Rose said, her eyes resting on her husband. "It's just knowing someone is there. Someone who cares about you."

Isaiah looked up from the floor, which he'd been

focused on while they talked. "I sure do care, Rosie. There ain't anyone could take your place. Ever."

"Well, hopefully, we'll have a whole bunch more years together. Now who's going to get those kinner down for bed tonight?"

"Not me," Isaiah said with a grin. "Their mamm's home now—thank the gut Lord."

Chapter Eight

The next morning, Beth got up early to help with breakfast before she planned to leave for home. She decided to stay for a while so she could talk to her sister about Josiah and to hear more about Anna's thoughts on marriage. She had strong reservations about Anna's obvious infatuation so early in her relationship with the man named Abe.

It was New Year's Eve day, but no one paid much attention to that holiday. Farmers couldn't take a day off from their animals just because the world wanted to celebrate. So everyone's day began and ended around the same time no matter what the calendar said.

Beth heard commotion coming from upstairs, which was nothing new since she'd been staying with her nephews. They came tripping down the stairs and collided with their grandmother, who had just removed fresh sticky buns from the oven. "Now, you almost knocked this tray out of my hand! You could have gotten burnt, Mark. Calm down."

"I wanna get outside and build a snowman with Matthew. I didn't mean to knock into you."

"Very well, but you need to eat breakfast first. Sit while I scramble up some eggs."

"I'll make them, Mamm," Beth said as she went into the refrigerator for butter.

"I like Grossmammi's better," Mark remarked as he took a seat on the bench next to the long trestle table.

"Too bad. I'm making them today," Beth said as she removed the bowl of fresh eggs and set them on the counter next to the stove.

"Well, I can—"

"Mamm, don't give into their demands. You aren't making it any easier for Anna."

"You're right. Okay, I'll start toast."

"I can't wait to go outside," Luke said as he walked over to the table.

"Why is that?" Rose asked her grandson.

"So I can throw snowballs at Mark and Matthew. My bruders are pains. They woke me up before the rooster."

Anna came down with Rachel beside her. "Where's Daed?"

"In your barn with Zach. They're gabbing before we head back home."

"He just tries to get away from my bruders," Rachel remarked, reaching for a glass of orange juice her aunt had poured earlier.

"Hey, that's mine," Mark said heading over to Rachel.

"Is not!"

"Whoa!" Beth turned around after breaking half a dozen eggs in a large bowl. "That's where your schwester always sits. If you want juice, just ask—nicely."

"May I pretty please have a little juice, dear Aenti?"

Beth rolled her eyes and looked over at Anna who was biting her lip to avoid smiling.

"I'll get it," Anna said as she reached for another juice glass. "So I bet you buwe had a gut time while I was away."

"Daadi made us work," Mark remarked as he reached for the juice.

"And you're going to continue to help your mudder, aren't you?" Rose said pointedly.

"Maybe."

"Oh yah, you remember what your daadi told you about Amish buwe learning to be hard workers even when they are young kinner."

"Jah, I remember. Luke's older. He should do most of the work."

"Work is shared," Rose continued with her lecture. "Then when many hands work together, no one does too much and the job gets done quick as a wink."

Anna smiled over at Mark. "We're going to have company next week-end so we'll have to get out chores done early in the week. The extra chores—not the daily ones."

"Who's coming here?"

"Well, a man named Abraham Stoltzfus and he's bringing his three children with him."

Luke looked up from his cereal. "Why do we have to have people stay here? That means you'll make me sleep with my bruders again."

"It shouldn't be a problem for a couple nights," Anna said. "Don't you want to hear about the kinner?"

"Not particularly," Luke said, returning to his cereal.

"Well, I'll tell you anyway. He has a bu just a little older than you, Luke. His name is John." She turned to Mark. "And he has another sohn named Benny, who will be turning nine in February."

Mark's eyes lit up. "Cool. Does he like softball?"

"I don't really know. You can ask him when he comes."

"It's too cold for a real game, Mark," Luke reminded him.

"Maybe not. We can hope. Or at least play catch. Matthew could join us."

"He ain't a gut catcher."

"But he has fun trying," Anna said.

She turned to her daughter. "And guess what? Abe has a daughter named Alice. We call her Allie."

"How old is she?"

"She will be four in April."

"Almost as old as me," Rachel said, grinning. "Can she stay in my room when she comes?"

"Of course. You have a big enough bed. She can sleep right alongside you."

"Does she like giraffes too?"

"Well, I really don't know. I know she plays with dolls."

"I hope she brings her own so she won't get mine all dirty."

"Selfish," Mark remarked under his breath as he reached for one of the sticky buns.

"They may still be hot, Mark. Be careful," his grandmother warned him.

"I'm glad everyone is gut about having company," Anna said, breathing a sigh of relief.

"Who said I'm happy?" Luke remarked with a smirk.

"Now, Sohn, we have to treat our guests with respect."

"Mmm."

"I mean it."

Beth looked over at her sister. "They'll be fine, Anna, if they know what's gut for them. Daadi will get a full report and so will Onkel Zach."

"We'll behave," Luke said, grimacing.

Oh how Anna hoped it would go well. If the children get along with each other, then they could work out any other details. It would be so nice to have a well-behaved family once again.

After Rose and Josiah packed up and left for their home, Beth stayed on with the pretense of wanting to help with the children for a while. In reality, she couldn't wait to get back to her own home and her privacy, but she was concerned about her sister's announcement about wanting to marry a man she barely knew.

When the children were all out playing, she and Anna sat at the kitchen table and had coffee and split a sticky bun. "Tell me more about Abe."

"I don't know what more to tell you. He's soft-spoken, though he handles his kinner real gut, and they respect him. I met his parents and his brother and—"

"You can get into his genealogy later, Anna. I want to know about him. Do you think you could handle the intimacy part?"

"He's not looking for that, Beth. He told me himself. At least not right away. Neither of us is."

"But a husband and a wife live close together. There is such a thing as desire—so I've heard anyway. Do you feel any 'desire' for the man?"

"Wow, you get right to the point. Let me say this. Nee, not desire that would lead to…you know. But I find him very attractive. He's actually handsome and he has a nice strong looking body—"

Beth let out a laugh. "Well, you seem to have given him the once-over."

"Well certainly I'm not going to be interested in a slob or a three-eyed monster!"

"It's okay," Beth said, trying to look serious. "You are a young woman and you have every right to look at the man, for Heaven's sake."

"When he touches me…like my hand… I kinda like it."

"I know. The human touch means so much." Beth looked down at her mug and swallowed hard to avoid tears. She wasn't a crier like so many women she knew, who cried if they saw a calf born, for heaven's sake, but lately her emotions were rather raw and at the surface.

Anna caught the drift of her sister's thoughts. "Beth, I'm so sorry I've been so self-centered. Mamm told me you broke up with Josiah. Do you want to talk about it?"

Beth looked up as she bit her lip. She nodded. "It hurts so bad. I really goofed up big time—again." She then proceeded to share her last day at the shop and she tried to remember every word spoken. Even the reciting of their conversation was difficult to bear. Her throat seemed to be closing in on her.

"Beth, it's okay to cry." Anna reached across and held her sister's hand. "I know."

Beth broke down and sobbed. She laid her head on her arms and allowed all the pain to be exposed. It helped. The tears helped. And knowing her dear sister loved her gave her hope that maybe one day someone else could love her as well.

"It sounds as if he was just hurt so bad he lost his temper. You said he'd had another relationship that fell apart."

"Jah, and he stayed away from women for a while so he wouldn't suffer again."

"Maybe in time, he can talk to you calmly and you can tell him how you really feel about him."

Beth nodded as she took a paper napkin and blew her nose. "It's too late for us. You should have seen him. I just have to get over him is all."

"Maybe. I think you shouldn't have quit. Now you won't see him at all, except at church service."

"I couldn't take his coldness. It was awful. We barely spoke. No job is worth that."

"It probably would have gotten better in time."

"Well, that's water over the dam. Now I just have to get over it and move on. No more men though. I'm done. I can't go through this again."

"Abe has a nice looking bruder and he's single," Anna said, smiling over at her sister.

"Anna! Are your ears blocked? I'm done!"

"I've heard that before."

"I mean it this time. I'd rather be single forever than go through this again. I have your kids to love and my other nieces and nephews. That should be enough."

Anna withdrew her hand and took a sip of coffee. "Not to change the subject, but I do want you to meet

Abe and his kinner next week-end. I could use your input."

"You don't think I'd miss it, do you? Goodness, I'm dying to meet him. I'll try to keep your buwe in line when I'm here, too."

"Denki. I'd appreciate any help you can give. Daed, too."

"And Zach. But in the end you'll have to let the kids spend time with each other alone so you can watch how they get along."

"And if they don't?"

"Then you'd better not marry. That could spell disaster."

"Jah, and I've had enough 'disaster' in my life. I don't need more." Anna tucked a loose strand of hair behind her kapp.

"I guess I'll go get Zach to take me home, Anna. He said he would be glad to. I could walk, but not with the roads as slippery as they are. It's starting to snow again. I'm ready for spring already and it's not even January yet."

"Tomorrow, though. The first day of the new year. Maybe both our lives will change for the good."

"That would be wonderful-gut."

New Year's day, Josiah spent the day alone, even though Lydia's mother had stopped by to invite him to join them for dinner. Maybe he should have accepted. It sure was quiet in his dark cluttered kitchen. After feeding the fire, he decided to work on his latest project. Though his heart wasn't in it, it would be wise to use his time fruitfully. It would also take the pressure off him to have it completed by the end of March as was requested.

The English family who had contracted the new kitchen were pleasant folk to work with, but they expected a new child in late April and wanted everything finished before the baby's arrival.

He still had several top cabinets to complete and then he planned to work on a matching cupboard to be installed across from their sink area. It was a large kitchen—over fifteen feet of cabinetry. Solid cherry.

After wiping down one of his worktables, he arranged the cut pieces in order and prepared to assemble the cabinet. There was a loud knock at the front door and he set his tools down and walked into the showroom. It was Beth's father, Isaiah. Goodness, perhaps there was some good news he wanted to share. He grinned widely as he unlocked the door and let Isaiah in.

"It's getting windy out there," Isaiah noted as he held a toot in his left hand and reached over for a handshake with his right. He stamped the snow off his boots on an entry mat for that purpose and stood at the door.

"Jah, hear we may get more snow before the end of the day. It snowed most of the night, I'm thinking," Josiah said.

"That's why I thought I'd better come by early, before the roads got real bad." He extended his hand holding the toot. "Here, Rose wanted you to have some of her famous sticky buns before they disappeared. She figured you'd be home today."

"That's real nice. Denki. They are mighty gut. Beth brought a couple when she worked here. I think

I gained two pounds in one afternoon. Would you like to sit down with me?"

"Nee, I have to get back, but speaking of Beth, she's been acting real sad lately and she won't talk about it. I was wondering if you could shed some light on things. You were gettin on real gut for a while. We were even thinking maybe things were serious between you two."

Josiah placed his thumbs behind his suspenders and rocked back and forth. "Did you ask your dochder?"

"I think Rosie tried to get her to talk, but when Beth wants to be silent, there ain't much one can do about it."

"I just don't want to say anything she'd be upset about. I can tell you this much, though. I loved your dochder and I probably still do, but we just can't seem to make it work. I'm afraid she has feelings for another man."

Isaiah's mouth dropped. "You're not talking about the English fellow she met at the market, are you?"

Josiah nodded.

"That weren't serious. She told me herself. They were just friends."

"It was more than that. And she was going to give him handmade gloves for Christmas. When that didn't work out so gut, she passed them on to me—without remembering to take out the note meant for him!"

"Mmm. I see. She's a foolish maed. Why she'd get involved with some English man, I can't fathom, Josiah. She should know better. I'm sure his motives weren't pure. I hope to Gott she didn't…"

"Me too. I'm not sure about anything anymore. But I won't be any woman's last resort."

"Nor should you be. You're a fine man, Josiah. I'd

better head back. I'm real sorry it didn't work out for you two. I would have been pleased to have you as my son-in-law."

"Denki. I appreciate that."

They shook hands again and then Josiah watched as Isaiah turned his buggy around in the parking lot and headed home. Once again the silence overwhelmed him. He walked slowly back to his project, even more depressed after their talk.

Chapter Nine

Anna checked the clock in the kitchen. Four o'clock on Thursday afternoon. In half an hour she planned to be waiting by her neighbor's phone for Abe's call, as pre-planned. She paced up and down the hallway from the front of the house to the kitchen, aware of dampness forming under her arms. Why was she so nervous? Goodness, it was just a call. *Jah*, but a very, very important call. Abraham Stoltzfus just might be her husband in the near future. That is, if he wasn't dissuaded by her unruly children.

So much hinged on the next day when he'd be arriving all the way from Holmes County, Ohio, for their families to meet. So much was riding on the next three days. Oh, if it were only over. No matter which way it went, she'd be able to breathe a sigh of relief just to know the outcome. Since she'd been home, she mulled over every word they'd spoken several times each day. She could picture his smile and hear his laugh. She was attracted to him, no doubt about it. But first and foremost, she knew him to be a good father, and discipline was sure needed in her home. Jeremiah had been a wonderful daed. Exemplary. No one could really take over his position in their household, but perhaps Abe could fill some of the void that Jeremiah's passing had left in all their lives.

Beth had promised to be here by now. The roads had cleared, so unless she'd forgotten, there shouldn't be a problem with her getting here. Anna never left the children alone. Normally, she'd drop them off at her sister-in-law's next door, but Lottie was supposed to stay off her feet due to swollen legs. She was in her eighth month of pregnancy with her sixth child and having some problems. Anna dropped off dinner for them each day around noon and she even took some of the laundry home with her to help out. Rose came by every afternoon to watch the children and Zach made sure he was available for naps and bedtimes. All in all, Lottie was taken care of, but Anna certainly wouldn't impose by adding her own tribe to the mix, even if it was only for an hour or so.

Rachel ran down the stairs where she'd been playing in her room. "I saw Aenti Beth's buggy coming in, Mamm. Can I go with you, wherever you're going?"

"Not this time, Rachel. I won't be long. I just have to talk on the phone to my friend who's coming tomorrow to make sure everything is settled."

"I hope they come. I cleaned up my old doll in case Allie doesn't bring her own."

"That's nice, honey. Real thoughtful."

"I'm better than my bruders, aren't I, Mamm? Luke is still grouchy about sharing his room. I think that's mean."

"I'd better have a talk with him one more time before they come. We Amish never mistreat others. It's really a sin."

"I even told him that," Rachel said, nodding. She folded her arms like an adult and scowled.

Beth appeared at the back door and Anna waved at her to come in. "Sorry, I was almost late. I was right in the middle of my latest book and lost track of time."

"You're here, that's all that matters," Anna said as her sister removed her boots and laid them on the boot mat.

"Hi, Rachel, how are you today?"

"Gut, except for my bruders."

"What's new."

"I guess I'll leave now so I won't have to rush. Help yourself to kaffi. It's fresh and I baked molasses cookies yesterday. Rachel, get some out of the cookie tin and place them on a plate for your aenti."

Beth shook her head. "Nee, I don't want any. I've had no appetite lately."

"Not even for cookies?"

Beth smiled. "Well, maybe just one. You do make the best."

Rachel took out two and handed one to Beth as she popped the other in her own mouth.

"I think you're supposed to ask, aren't you?" Beth said, cocking her head to the side as she looked at her niece.

"Oh, I forgot. Mamm, can I have a cookie?"

Anna laughed. "What if I say no?"

"I'd have to spit it out and that would be wasteful. I remember all about the kinner who are starving."

"Oh, I see. That's convenient. You can have one

more, but drink a glass of milk with it. Now I really must run."

"Where are the monsters? I mean your buwe?" Beth asked as Anna placed her heaviest shawl on her shoulders and covered her prayer kapp with her black bonnet.

"They're upstairs, supposedly cleaning their rooms for their guests, but they've been way too quiet. You can check them if you want."

"You go. I may check them or I may just sit and talk to your dochder."

When Anna got to the phone shanty, she nodded to an elderly man who was just leaving. She checked her watch and realized she still had five minutes to wait. She took several deep breaths, blowing the air out through puckered lips—ever so slowly to calm herself down. It seemed to work and when the phone rang, she picked it up before it gave its second ring. "Hullo?"

"Anna, is that you?" She recognized Abe's voice immediately. Deep, gentle, manly.

"Jah, it's me. Right on time—just like you want."

He laughed and she pictured his handsome face.

"You're right. You're nice and punctual. How have you been?"

"Gut. I had a nice ride home. No problems. How are you and your kinner?"

"We're gut too. We finished up the cake the day you left. It was real yummy. I bet I gained weight."

"Well, you look nice any way," she said, feeling moisture gather under her arms again from her nerves. "So you still coming tomorrow?"

"Jah, if you can have us. My cousins were excited that we're coming."

"I hope your kinner can stay with us. We're redding up the rooms upstairs, just in case."

"They'd love that. You sure it won't be too much?"

"Nee. The kinner are real excited." *Well, maybe not Luke—yet.*

"I'm not sure about Allie. Naomi keeps talking to her about it, but so far, she gets upset every time it's mentioned."

"Aw, that's a shame. Whatever works out, Abe, that's fine with me."

"Well, I figured, maybe you can come here in a couple weeks again. I think it's important that we see each other as much as possible before making a decision. What do you think?"

"I agree. And maybe this week-end won't go so gut, but we shouldn't give up too soon."

He was silent for a moment. "I'm sure it will go just fine."

"I meant with the kinner. They may have to work through some things, you know."

"I suppose you're right. Well, I'd better get back home. We'll probably get in around four. We'll have supper with my cousins and then head over."

"Why don't you come here for supper? I'll make macaroni and cheese and hot dogs. All kids like that."

"It won't be too much?"

"Abe, you forget—I'm Amish. We're born with wooden spoons in our hands."

He laughed again. "Not silver spoons in our mouths?"

She giggled. "Not this Amish girl."

"Have a gut evening, Anna. We'll see you tomorrow."

She hung up and sighed from relief. It went so well. He sounded just as interested as when they parted. Now to go home and begin the lecture once more on Amish manners.

When Abe got back to his home, he found John sitting on the sofa doing a crossword puzzle. "John, you need to have everything ready tonight. The driver will be here first thing in the morning."

"I don't know why we have to go all the way to Pennsylvania just to meet more people."

"I told you before, it's important to get to know Anna Miller and her whole family."

"You'll probably marry her even if we hate her kinner."

"That's a terrible thing to say. Hate is a very strong and ugly word. I don't want to hear it again from your mouth."

"You know what I mean, Daed. Maybe not hate, but what if they're weird or something."

"Let's just wait and see. I'm sure they're a lot like you are. They've been raised with the same values in the same kind of community."

"What if you marry her, Daed? Would we have to move?"

"I've been thinking that one over, Sohn. Anna and I would have to talk it over before deciding. I imagine she'd be willing to move here since I have my farm all established."

"And if she doesn't want to?"

"Let's not discuss all the possibilities now. Just pack

enough clothing for three nights. Clean underwear and socks for one thing."

"And my toothbrush, I know, even though I hate to use it."

"It's important. You don't want to lose all your teeth when you're older."

"Who's packing for Benny?"

"He can pack for himself. Where did he go anyway?"

"He's outside checking on the new goat. He's crazy about that kid."

"I'll go get him in a minute. I just want to make sure you know how important it is to make a gut impression this week-end. You're a great young man, but I know you aren't real excited about all this. Please don't make it difficult for me."

"I won't. I'll try to be nice to everyone, even if it kills me."

Abe pressed his shoulder affectionately. "Denki. I hope everything works out. I can't tell you how much it would mean to have us all together again. Allie's breaking my heart."

"Just tell her she has to come home."

"It's not that easy, Sohn. Someday when you're a daed, you'll understand."

"That's not for a long, long time," he said. "And I'm glad I'm just a kid. Maedel can be pretty tough."

"Oh jah, that's for sure."

"And for certain," his son added with a grin.

Chapter Ten

Naomi held Allie in her arms as the boys climbed into the hired car. Abe came over to his daughter and sister, hoping Allie might still change her mind about coming. Allie quickly turned her head and buried it in her aunt's apron top.

"There's no use, Abe. She's not going with you."

He nodded. "Then I'll talk Anna into coming here again soon. The whole point of this arrangement is to get Allie back with the buwe and me."

"I know she's the main reason you're thinking marriage, but you have the buwe to consider too. They need a mudder as well—ever so much. Now go and enjoy your time away. You know we'll take gut care of your dochder."

He leaned over and kissed Naomi on the cheek and patted his daughter's head. "See you soon, Allie. Be gut for Aenti Naomi."

Without turning, she made a slight nod.

"Hurry up, Daed. It's getting late," Benny called out from the car.

Abe climbed in front with the driver and as they pulled away, everyone waved. Allie turned and grinned at her family, waving vigorously. Their driver, Tom, looked over at Abe. "She's a cute kid. She'll come around. Give her time."

"Jah, I sure hope so. I may as well tell you why I'm going to Pennsylvania. There's a nice Amish lady there, a widow, who might be willing to take on my family as well as her own."

"Well, that sounds mighty nice. Yup, you've had a hard time of it, Abe. I'd like to see you get a little happiness out of your life."

"It's not for me, Tom."

"Maybe that's not your first concern, but you're a young man yet. You have needs of your own."

The boys were listening intently and began giggling.

"Uh, I guess we'll discuss this at another time," Tom said, peering at them through the rear view mirror. "I meant like meals and clean clothes, and…"

"Jah. I know. So you've made this trip before, I guess."

"To Lancaster County? Probably only a hundred times," Tom said grinning.

The men chatted on about sports and even politics, though Abe only knew about the major current events. He was too busy caring for his family's needs to spend time gathering information about the outside world. Some of his friends enjoyed keeping up with national politics, but Abe preferred to read about increasing crop yields or ways to irrigate.

In the beginning of the trip the boys entertained

themselves with UNO and other card games and then went through the alphabet by reading letters from billboards. Throughout the rest of the trip John became fairly quiet, even when they stopped to eat lunch. Abe feared there could be a problem with John accepting a new woman in their home.

He prayed frequently that his boys would accept Anna and her family if it was decided to go through with a marriage. He kept going back to their meeting and the amazing way God had brought them together. If God could do that, surely melding the two sets of children into one family would be a piece of cake. Their meeting had seemed providential.

Around half past three, Tom pulled up to Abe's cousin Mo's house. They lived on the edge of Lititz and ran a small stand in good weather where they sold produce and handmade bird houses. It supplemented the income Mo made from his crops and gave his father, who lived with them, something to do with his spare time. Due to a farming accident years before, his father was no longer able to run the family farm. Mo's parents lived in the attached dawdi-haus where his mother encouraged her husband's woodworking hobby. She claimed it kept him busy and away from the kitchen, thereby making her life easier. They were a lively couple and Abe enjoyed seeing them again.

It had been over a year since he and his family had stayed with Mo to attend the funeral of a family member in Lancaster. Of course Mary and his two other sons and dear Ruthie were alive at the time. Certainly felt strange to be there without them, but he forced himself to put those thoughts aside.

After chatting for an hour, Mo gave them direc-

tions to Anna's place. He had known Jeremiah from
attending auctions together and had even met Anna
once. He told Abe to take their second buggy and use
it any time he wanted.

As Abe headed over to Anna's, the boys sat in the
back and were silent the whole distance. "You guys
okay back there?"

"Fine," John answered.

"Jah, it's nice," Benny added.

"Awful quiet."

"Not much to say, Daed," John said.

"I'm kinda excited," Benny said, "though maybe a
little scared, too."

Abe laughed. "Scared of what?"

"Maybe Anna's kinner won't like me."

John looked over at his brother. "Don't be silly.
There's nothing wrong with you."

"You say that cuz you're my bruder."

Abe chimed in. "Nee, he says that because it's true.
You're a nice Amish bu. You're caring and smart and
gut at pitching."

"Not so gut catching though," Benny added, lips
turned down.

"Well maybe you can play with the maed then,"
John teased.

"Their place should be coming up pretty soon," Abe
said as he slowed down the horse. "Cousin Mo told me
it will be on our right and there's a windmill in the
front and a large oak tree behind the house."

"I see it, Daed! It's the next one, I'm sure." Benny
was all excited and leaned forward to get a better view.

"We'll check the name on the mailbox," Abe said
as they drew closer.

John leaned over beside his brother. "Jah, it says 'Miller.' Of course there are probably a hundred Millers along this road."

"Nee, I'm sure that's it." Abe turned the horse's reins and headed down the drive. "Nice place," he added as he made his way toward the large barn. A man was just closing the door. "Huh, maybe it ain't the right house. I didn't expect a man to be here." Abe felt a pit in his stomach.

The stranger waved and then pointed to a spot beside the barn where there was a post for hitching. After Abe stopped the horse, the three of them got out of the buggy. The man came over and introduced himself. "I'm Anna's bruder—Zach. Nice to meet you," he said, extending his hand. Abe relaxed and shook his hand.

"Nice to meet you too. These are my buwe, John and Ben."

Zach smiled and shook their hands as well. Ben stood a little straighter.

"My schwester is expecting you. I'd stay, but I need to get home to check on my kinner. Just go to the back and knock on the door. I'm sure Anna's still working in the kitchen."

"Denki. Hope to see you again."

"Jah, I'm sure you will."

Before going further, Abe spoke to his boys. "Get your bags with your clothes, buwe. You know you're staying here."

"I wish you were staying here, too," Benny remarked as he turned towards the buggy.

"I wish this was over and I was home," John remarked as he joined his brother.

"Now remember what I've told you about being polite."

"Jah, Daed. We remember," John added, his expression grim.

As they approached the kitchen door, Matthew swung it open and gave a huge smile. "Hi. I'm Matthew."

Benny grinned back. "Jah, I figured that's who you were. Your mamm told me about you guys."

"I'm John. Benny's big bruder," John said with little expression on his thin face.

"Yah, you look bigger and older," Matthew said, nodding.

"Gut to meet you," Abe said to Anna's middle son, as he held out his hand.

Matthew grinned as he accepted a handshake. "My Mamm is all nervous. Come on in. I think she's upstairs."

When they came in, Anna appeared descending the stairs. Her cheeks were flushed and she went right over to Abe's boys. "I see you met Matthew already. Luke and Mark are still cleaning their rooms, but they'll be right down to meet you."

Abe smiled over as he closed the door behind them. "Hi, Anna. You have a nice place here. You keep it real neat."

"I try, but my bruder Zach helps me a lot with the outside work. Oh, and so do my kinner. Where's my dochder?" Anna looked around and then called out. Rachel had been hiding out in the sitting room, but she came into the kitchen when she heard her mother call her. "This is Rachel," Anna added, placing her hands on her daughter's shoulders.

"Hi," she said weakly.

They replied and then everyone turned as Mark and Luke came racing down the stairs, trying to be the first one down. Anna caught her breath. Not a very good beginning.

Abe just smiled and introduced his children and himself to the rambunctious young boys.

"Do you want to show John and Ben where they'll be staying tonight?" Anna suggested.

"Jah," Luke said first. "You'll be with me, John, cuz we're about the same age. Do you like baseball?"

"Jah, it's okay," he answered as he reached down for his bag of clothes and followed Luke to his room. Then Matthew and Benny followed them up. Mark stood staring at Abe.

"Don't you want to go with the buwe?" Anna asked her son.

"If I have to."

"Mark! Bitte. Remember what we talked about."

Mark let out a sigh. "All right." He turned towards the stairs and walked slowly up to the bedrooms.

Rachel looked disappointed and Anna realized her daughter had hoped to meet Allie. Turning to Abe she asked about his daughter.

"I'm sorry she didn't come with us." He turned to Rachel. "My Allie is real shy. She didn't want to come this time, but next time we're together, I'm sure she'll want to come play with you."

"Okay." She looked down at the floor. "I had a dolly ready for her to play with."

"That's very thoughtful of you. I'll be sure to tell her."

"Is she as big as me?"

"She's a little younger. Not quite four yet. I'm sure you're bigger."

"I like little people. I help my aenti take care of her boppli and she's going to have another one real soon. Right Mamm?"

Anna smiled at her daughter. "Jah, real soon and I'm sure we'll be there to help out."

"I hope *you* have a boppli soon, too, Mamm. It would be ever so much fun."

Anna felt the flush travel from her neck to her cheeks. Goodness, her daughter sure knew how to embarrass her.

Abe couldn't hold back a grin, but he remained silent.

"Now, go upstairs and play by yourself till supper is ready, Rachel."

"Okay," she said as she left reluctantly.

"I have everything nearly ready for supper. Are you hungry?" she asked Abe as she pointed to a chair for him.

He sat down and nodded. "I hope it's not too much for you."

"Of course not." She turned the hotdogs sizzling on the iron fry pan and then sat across from Abe. "How was your trip?"

"Gut. Pretty country. Anna, you look kinda nervous. Please try to relax. Everything will be just fine."

"I guess I am a bit nervous. I've tried to prepare you for my buwe. They are really quite a strain."

"They've been through a lot, just as you have. It will take time to settle them down maybe."

"I've about given up."

"Maybe that's why Gott brought me here. To help you through these times."

"Abe, I'm hoping that's it. It would be ever so nice to have gut buwe again. When Jeremiah…"

"Jah, I know it was easier when you weren't alone trying to raise them. So let me look around. You keep a nice kitchen, Anna. Smells gut in here, too."

"I have cookies."

"Nee, not before I eat. I want to do justice to your macaroni and cheese. It's one of my favorite dishes. Mary used to…"

"Goodness, we're kinda living in the past still, aren't we?" Anna said, trying not to show the pain of her memories. It was strange to have a man sitting where Jeremiah had so often sat. Could she actually deal with marriage so soon?

"I'll show you the sitting room and the basement if you want," she said, rising.

"Oh jah, I like basements," he said grinning at her.

"I guess that was silly."

"Nee, I really do. And attics, too."

Anna let out a laugh, feeling her body start to relax. "I have one of them too, but it's a mess."

"Attics are supposed to be messy. They're more fun that way."

"I guess we'll save part of the tour for another day. Supper is just about ready." She showed him through the first floor rooms and then called the children for supper. Surprisingly, they walked down the stairs instead of running, and except for Mark and John, everyone seemed in good spirits.

Rachel barely said a word throughout the meal, but

she looked over at Abe several times as well as his boys and appeared satisfied with what she saw.

Anna prayed silently as the food was passed around for the second time. She received comfort from her prayers and began to smile more—and worry less. Maybe everything would go just fine after all.

Chapter Eleven

Josiah decided to pick up on his Greek lessons once again. He had to do something besides carpentry or mope around feeling sorry for himself. Life does go on even when someone breaks your heart. It was time to try to translate some of the early writings from the Greek to English. After all, he'd been doing the basic grammar for over a year now and it was a bit monotonous.

After closing the shop early one Saturday afternoon, he took the buggy into Lititz. After tethering his driving horse to a post, he went into the library. He looked around amazed at all the rows and rows of reading material. It excited him to think so many people had taken the time to share their thoughts and experiences on paper so complete strangers, like himself, could learn from them or be transported into other worlds through their imaginations.

A young librarian was seated at a desk behind a counter. She was in such deep concentration, that it was several moments before she realized he was standing there.

"Oh, I'm sorry. I didn't see you waiting. I hope you weren't here long." Her dark brown hair was cropped short, accenting her large almond-shaped blue eyes. She was dressed in black pants with a teal green sweater.

"Nee, not long. I'm afraid I've never been in here before so I don't know where to begin looking."

Observing his Amish dress, she asked if he was looking for books on agriculture.

"Nee, actually not. I've been studying Greek and I think I'm ready to start reading simple texts now in the language. Do you have some early writings? Maybe Plato or Socrates?"

"Oh, my. No one's ever asked for ancient Greek writings. I don't think there is anything. We're small, you know. Maybe I can check with the other libraries and—"

"I don't want to put you through all that. I'll check out some of the stores that sell used books in the area. Maybe I'll find something there which I can keep."

"You're quite unusual, you know." She smiled sweetly at him, causing him to wish he'd scrubbed up better before coming in.

"Oh just because I'm Amish doesn't mean I'm not interested in other things."

"I'm sure. I didn't mean to insult you, it's just…well, I never met an Amishman who wanted to read in another language, other than German, you know. How about if I go on line right now and see what some of the on-line prices would be."

"I'm sure you're much too busy."

"No, I'm not, really. I'm bored stiff as a matter-of-fact. You're only the fifth person who's come in today."

He grinned. Noting a chair by the side of her desk, he asked with his eyes if he could sit and she nodded towards the chair. "Yes, by all means. Relax while I check out a few sites."

He sat and observed this charming woman seated across from him. She certainly was pretty and very friendly.

"Yes, I thought so. This is a good site for you." She turned the screen so he could read it and pointed out several classical books available for sale at reasonable prices.

"Huh. Amazing. At those prices, I could start quite a library. Let me take down some notes."

"Do you have access to a computer?" she asked.

"I use one in my work. I own a carpentry shop." When he told her the location, she raised her brows.

"My goodness, I live with my parents only about a mile from there. I pass it every day on my way to work."

"Really? Small world, ain't—isn't it? I can't use the Internet though. It's against the rules so I'd have to have someone else order them for me or—"

"I'd be more than happy to help you out. I could get the information, print it out, and drop it off on my way back from work. Then if you want to order something, I could help you do that as well."

"That's really nice of you, uh…" He looked around the desk for a name plate, but seeing none, looked at her inquisitively.

"Nicole. Nicole Morrison. And you are?" she asked as she extended her hand for a handshake.

"Josiah Yoder," he said as he reached for her hand. His large hand enveloped her slender fingers and he quickly withdrew his hand. "Did I hurt you? I'm so sorry if I did."

"No no. I'm fine. I'm not as fragile as I look. I have a twin brother and we spent many an hour wrestling or climbing trees. I'm pretty strong actually."

He laughed. "I wouldn't have believed it. You're so…so feminine looking."

"That's what I've been told."

A teen-age girl came to the desk with several books to check out. Nicole moved to the side and took care of her and then returned and sat down.

"So what do you think? Do you want me to research this some more and leave the information off for you tomorrow or the next day?"

"That would be wonderful-gut. I'd really appreciate it. Socrates might be too difficult for me at this stage, but I need something challenging. I've been so busy in my new business that I've let everything else slide."

"I know what you mean. It's easy to do. I've taken up quilting and every evening I can't wait to get at it. I dream patches."

He laughed. "I don't know how you maedel make such tiny little stitches. My mamm makes amazing designs when she does her quilts. I have one on my bed." That was way too personal to discuss. He cleared his throat and looked over at a bookcase behind her desk.

She followed his eyes. "Those are the returns from the last three days. I guess I'd better get busy or I'll hear about it from my boss."

"I thought you were your own boss. I don't see anyone else here."

"Oh, Miss Knight is away until Monday. I love it when I'm alone here. By the way, I need a small table for my bedroom so I can have a lamp for reading. Maybe you could design something for me. Sometimes, I like to be alone when I read. It's easier when there aren't interruptions. Know what I mean?"

"Oh jah. When I work, I like to have it quiet. Even though it's lonely sometimes, if it's too silent."

"So you're not married."

"Nee. And you?"

"Not even near. I'm in no rush. Too many of my friends rushed into marriage and now they're sorry, or divorced. Not me. When I do marry, it has to be for a lifetime."

"I believe the same."

"Yes, I know you Amish don't divorce."

"It's very rare."

"Good for you."

"Well, I'd better give you a chance to put those books where they belong," he said nodding towards the shelf, partially loaded with the returned books.

She let out a sigh. "It's more fun to talk to someone. Someone interesting anyway. You'll see me again, Josiah. I'll work on the information for you, probably even tonight."

"Instead of quilting?" he asked with a crooked smile.

"Well, maybe in addition," she said, coyly smiling back.

After he left, he headed back to his shop. So Beth Beachy isn't the only maed in the world. Obviously, this wasn't going to go very far, but it was fun to have a girl to talk to. And a pretty one at that.

* * *

Abe sat with Anna while she washed up the dishes from supper. He offered to help, but she refused his offer. "Nee, just keep me company."

"I think the kinner seem to like each other, don't you?" Abe asked as he leaned back in the wooden chair and stretched his legs under the table.

"Yah, it's going pretty gut. But then it hasn't been very long. We'll see tomorrow. It's supposed to warm up a bit. I was hoping they could play in the snow together. Maybe build a snowman or something."

"It wonders me how you manage so gut," Abe said, looking around the neat kitchen.

"Sometimes my family helps out."

"And I guess the buwe have chores."

"They do. Luke takes care of our cow, Barbie. Milks her twice a day."

"And the little ones?"

"They have to keep the kindling stacked, collect the eggs, little things. And they will all help me in my vegetable garden this spring—even Rachel."

"That's gut. They need to feel part of the family and know they're productive."

Anna smiled. "So far, it hasn't been too bad?"

"Not at all. Have you been thinking anymore about marriage?"

She nodded. It was difficult to use the words.

"Did you mention it to your kinner?" he asked.

"Jah. Luke wasn't real excited about the idea, but he'll come around, I'm thinking."

"It helps to spend time together."

Luke came charging down from the second floor where the boys were playing together. He went straight to Anna's side. "John threw my pillow on the floor and won't pick it up."

Abe stood up and started to walk to the stairs, at which point, a red-faced John appeared on the staircase, heading his way.

"I just wanted to try his bed, Daed, that's all and he had a fit."

Abe turned towards Luke. "Is that true?"

"But he didn't have to take the pillow off and put it on the floor. It'll get dirty."

Abe looked at John and scowled. "Why would you put it on the floor anyway? It wasn't your place to just take over Luke's bed now, was it?"

"I knew you'd take his side." John glared over at Luke. "You can have your lousy bed. I brought my own sleeping bag. And my own pillow."

"Oh, dear." Anna stood alongside Abe, wondering what to say.

"Maybe I'll have John sleep at my cousin's tonight. That way we won't get into any more conflicts," Abe said, disappointment showing in his eyes.

"He could sleep downstairs in the sitting room on the floor or the sofa," Anna said weakly.

"Well, let's think about it."

The boys were standing absolutely still, looking at each other the way two stags do competing for a doe.

"How about if we all sit and chat? Or play a board game together," Anna suggested, her voice wavering.

"I hate board games," Luke said.

"No you don't," Anna remarked. "You often play Monopoly. Why don't we set it up here in the kitchen?"

"Well, I'm not playing," Luke informed them.

"Neither am I," John added.

"Then sulk. The two of you," Abe said, obviously annoyed with them both. "Just don't get into any more trouble. I won't have it."

Luke glared and for a moment, Anna held her breath, fearing the next words out of her son's mouth. Fortunately, he merely turned and went back upstairs. John stayed down and sat in the sitting room, staring straight ahead, arms folded. Abe shrugged and nodded towards the kitchen. "Silence is golden."

She smiled slightly and went back to her dishes. "How much snow do you have in Ohio?" she asked.

"About the same as you do here. By the way, supper was real gut, Anna. Denki."

"It was just macaroni and cheese and hot dogs. Not exactly exciting."

"Exciting doesn't do it at my home. Everyday food is what goes over with my buwe. Plain cooking."

She smiled over. "Plain food for us Plain folk. Makes sense." She dried the last dish and put it away. "It's too dark to show you around the farm. Maybe tomorrow. What time will you come by?"

"Is one too early?"

"Oh, that's late. I want you for our dinner. Zach butchered a deer last week and I planned on making venison pot roast for everyone."

"Sounds gut. I'll have to tell Mo and his fraa not to expect us then."

Rachel came into the kitchen, tears streaming down her cheeks. "My bruders won't let me play with them. Matthew and Mark want Benny all to themselves."

"Well you just tell them it ain't right to exclude you," Anna said. "What are they playing?"

"I think it's called arm wrestling."

Abe and Anna looked at each other and grinned. "Honey," Anna started, "That's really for buwe, don't you think? They'd be too strong for you and you might get hurt."

"I'm strong, too," she said as she held up one arm, pushed her sleeve up beyond her elbow and flexed an invisible muscle. "See?"

Abe smiled at her. "You are real strong, I can see that, but your mamm is right. Buwe are stronger than they look and they don't always think about what they're doing. Why don't you stay here with us instead?"

"I saw John sitting by himself. Maybe he'll play with me." She turned and went towards the sitting room.

"This should be interesting," Abe said under his breath.

He and Anna tiptoed to the edge of the kitchen where they could hear what transpired.

"I don't play dolls," John was saying.

"But we could play house and you could be the daed and I—"

"Look, I don't want to hurt your feelings, but I don't play house either."

"What do you play?" Annoyance was apparent in her question.

"Well, do you play chess?"

"Nee."

"Checkers?"

"Yah, and I beat my mamm sometimes."

"All right. Get the checkers, but just one game, okay?"

"Goody!" They could hear her sorting through the games, so they returned to their seats in the kitchen.

"John is such a nice bu. Not many buwe his age would play checkers with a little maed."

"He gets along real gut with Allie—when she's with us. Which isn't often." He looked down at the table cloth and traced the checkered squares with his finger.

"I'm so sorry, Abe. Maybe that will change."

"It has to, Anna. I'll be truthful with you. If she doesn't want to come home when you're at our place, I'm afraid…"

"So far, she seems to like me," Anna said softly.

He looked up and smiled. "Jah, I believe she does. Can you come next week-end, so she'll get to know you better? That's the main thing for me. I want her to stay overnight while you're there, to see how things work out. She needs to return to our home before I do anything permanent."

"I understand. My buwe have to adjust to the idea too. Hopefully, after this week-end, we'll have more assurance it could work out."

"It may take a while."

"Jah, but of course it's important for you and me to get to know each other better, too," Anna said.

"I'm not afraid of our relationship. I know you to be a fine Amish woman."

"Abe, you barely know me. I have a temper, sometimes."

"Don't we all?"

"Amish women aren't supposed to."

Abe laughed. "Tell that to my mamm."

She grinned. "I wouldn't dare."

"I can lose my temper, too, Anna, though I try not

to. It never helps a situation to start yelling. Parenting takes a lot of self-discipline, I've discovered. My Mary used to lash out sometimes something fierce, but it never lasted long. She was basically even-tempered."

"Lash out at the kinner? Or you?" Anna asked with a smile.

"Both. She hated it when I forgot to take off my work boots—especially when she'd just redded up the kitchen floor."

"Well, yah," Anna said, raising her brows. "My goodness, why are men so careless. Jeremiah used to do the same thing."

"Anything else he used to do that frustrated you?"

She sat silent a moment, memories running through her head. "At night, he liked to brush my hair and sometimes he pulled it too hard and made it hurt."

"I see. I'll put that on my list of 'don'ts' then. No hair pulling. Anything else?"

"He never finished his spinach."

"Maybe he didn't like spinach."

"He didn't, but you should still eat it all."

"I guess so. I don't like Brussel sprouts. Will I have to eat my whole serving?" His smile turned up on one side.

"I'll make it small, just to help you out," she answered, grinning back.

Rachel returned to the kitchen, this time with a pleasant expression. "I beat John," she said.

"Doesn't he want a re-match?" Abe asked.

"Not now, but he said maybe tomorrow. He just went upstairs. He said he'd sleep on the floor in the sitting room."

"Well, that's gut," Anna said. "At least he's willing to stay here."

"Jah," Abe added, nodding. "That's a gut sign. I hope we'll see more gut signs before the week-end is over."

Rachel walked over to his chair and leaned against his arm. "I like your family. I hope Allie comes next time."

Anna breathed easier. At least she could count on her daughter.

Chapter Twelve

Beth and her parents headed over to Anna's around three the next afternoon.

"I hope we like this Abe fellow," her mother said from the front seat.

Beth looked out the side window and remained silent.

"What do you know about him, Beth, besides him being a widower?"

"Not much. She thinks he's nice."

"Well, I'd hope so."

"Sure seems we'll find out mighty soon," Isaiah said looking straight ahead at the road. "It appears to be part of Gott's plan, the way they met and all."

"If that's the case, it can't fail," Rose said.

Beth nodded. She wished God had someone in mind for her. For a while, she figured Josiah was the right man.

Free will. That's what kind of goofed up those plans. It apparently had been her will to get involved with

Randy, and look where that got her. Not only was that utter foolishness, but it led to the breakup of her friendship with Josiah. If only she'd remembered to remove the note from the gloves. Oh, well. It's done with, and she had to accept it.

Right now, her main concern was her job. She needed one. There simply wasn't enough to do in the winter. Cooking, preserving, and quilting—all the things Amish women appeared to enjoy, she found monotonous and boring.

Maybe she'd check out the help wanted ads in Lititz. The county kept the roads pretty clear so she could probably make it in to work most days; but where could she work there? One thing was for sure and certain, it wouldn't be a bank!

As they pulled into Anna's drive they saw the children playing in the yard. There were two snowmen in the process of being built. The boys had just added an old straw hat to the top of their snowman, who stood nearly five feet high. Anna and Abe, along with Rachel, were rolling something that appeared to be the head for their shorter snow figure.

After tethering the horse, Beth and her parents got out and walked towards the group. Anna and Abe came right over with his sons. Since their mittens were covered with wet snow, they just nodded at Beth and her parents as they were introduced.

"I'll go put on kaffi," Anna suggested. "We waited till you came to have dessert. Besides, I'm freezing."

Abe grinned and nodded. "I'll come in in a few minutes. I just want to help Rachel finish up her snowman."

"It's gonna be a snow*maed*," Rachael reminded him.

"Oh, jah, I forgot. We'll need something for her head."

"I have an old bonnet I was going to get rid of. I'll look for it," Anna said as she and her family headed for the back door.

"Mamm, do you have an extra carrot for her nose?" Rachel called after her.

"I'm sure I can come up with one."

Mark yelled over and asked for one for their snowman.

John sat down on a large rock crossing his arms over his knees. He appeared bored by the whole venture.

After Luke poked broken branches in the side of the belly for arms, he went over and sat on the rock next to John, though neither said a word.

Anna was dying to see how they interacted, but the cold penetrated through her old jacket causing major discomfort. Besides, she knew her father would be ready for coffee and a goody about now.

When they got inside, everyone hung up their outer garments on hooks by the stove. While Anna started coffee in her large granite-wear pot on the back of the stove, Beth took out paper napkins and small dessert plates, along with forks. "The pumpkin pies look gut. When did you make them?" she asked her sister.

"Early this morning. Abe helped me mix the pumpkin. So what do you think everyone? Isn't he nice?"

"Goodness, Anna, we were just introduced," Rose said. "We barely know the man."

"He's nice looking. I'll say that for him," Beth said as she went to get cream from the refrigerator.

"Oh, jah, he is," Anna said, smiling over.

"Of course, looks aren't everything. Look at Josiah.

He wasn't exactly handsome, but he was certainly a nice man. Interesting too." Had those words come out of Beth's mouth? Goodness, why was she still talking about the man. He was *history!*

No one said a word. After a full minute passed, Anna went to the back porch and rang the bell. It would be several minutes before there'd be a response from the kinner. She was sure of that, but it was too cold for them to remain out there much longer. Especially Rachel, who had awakened with a runny nose.

Several minutes later, all six of the children went through the utility room, dumping their wet boots and mittens, before arriving in the kitchen. Most looked happy. But not John or Luke. Even Abe's mouth was rigid.

Something had transpired, but it was not to be shared at that moment. Anna's eyes connected with Abe's and he changed his stern expression into a half-hearted smile. "That kaffi smells gut. We get to try your pies now, right?" he asked Anna.

"Jah, that's for sure. Kids, do you want pie or ice cream?"

They all wanted the pie *with* ice cream, so Beth and Anna worked together while Abe made conversation with their parents. Isaiah asked about Abe's farm and his livestock while Rose sat quietly and smiled.

Matthew, Mark and Benny raced through their dessert and then excused themselves to build a city with the Legos in the sitting room. Rachel sat next to her grandmother, who extended her shawl to include the blue-lipped child. Rachel's teeth were chattering. "Goodness, little one, you should have come in sooner."

"I wanted to stay with the buwe. They were having so much fun."

"I hope you don't get sick," Anna said as she laid dessert in front of her.

"Her head feels warm, Anna," her mother noted. "Feel it."

Anna reached over and placed her warm hand on Rachel's forehead. "Jah, it does. I'll take her temperature later."

Abe looked over at them. "I'm sorry, I didn't even notice how cold she was. I should have brought her in sooner."

"Nee, it was my fault," Anna said quickly. "I'm the mudder. I should have known better."

Rachel's eyes filled. "I don't wanna be sick. I wanna play with the kinner. It ain't fair."

Anna took her in her arms. "Now honey, you can watch from the sofa. I just don't want you to get close to anyone, if you're coming down with something."

Rachel burrowed her head in her mother's chest and cried. John walked in at that moment and looked at the sobbing child. "What's wrong?"

"Apparently, Rachel has a bad cold and may be running a fever," Abe answered. "She shouldn't have been out in the cold, but no one realized."

"That's too bad," John said as he patted Rachel on her shoulder.

She turned her head so she could see him and gave him a feeble smile—but a smile just the same. "You're nice. Nicer than my bruders."

This brought smiles to the others—John included.

"When you feel up to it, I'll challenge you to a game of checkers."

"Jah? Oh, boy, I think I'm getting better already."

"I want you to change into warmer clothes, Rachel. Go upstairs now. I'll come up and take your temperature."

A couple minutes later, Anna excused herself and went up to take care of Rachel.

Beth sat across from Abe as John took a seat next to his father. "So, Abe, you have a younger dochder, too?" Beth asked as she swallowed a bite of the pie.

"Jah. Allie. I was hoping she'd come, too, but she's real shy."

"How old is she? I know Anna told me, but I can't remember."

"She's nearly four. She's grown very close to my schwester ever since…"

Beth nodded. "I understand. Anna hasn't mentioned where you'd be living if you two get married. Have you made a decision yet?"

Her parents looked over silently, waiting for his answer.

"Uh, we haven't gotten that far yet, Beth. We need to talk about it, but it's really too early. First off, we have to see how our kinner get along with each other."

John sat staring straight ahead. Abe leaned over and suggested his son check on his brother. Reluctantly, he rose and left the room.

"There will always be problems at first, don't you think?" Beth asked, studying his expression.

"Now, Beth," her father broke in, "You don't have to give the poor man the third degree."

"Is that what I'm doing?" Her face flushed. She

licked her lips. "I'm sorry. Anna means the world to me and I just don't want her hurt. She's been through too much already."

Abe looked down at his empty plate and pushed the fork around. "We've both been through a lot, Beth. No one wants to get hurt, but we have to be cautious. We can't just jump into a marriage without thinking it through very carefully. There are too many factors, the kinner being our main concern."

"I'm sure you and Anna will make the right decision. Again, I shouldn't have said anything. Please accept my apology."

"None needed. Of course you are concerned for your schwester." He looked over at Isaiah and Rose, who were silently watching the exchange. "I can tell you this though, if we do marry, I'll do everything in my power to take gut care of Anna and her kinner. She's a very sweet lady and I would never want to hurt her."

Isaiah pulled on his beard and stared into Abe's eyes. "I believe you. I hope Gott sees fit to put you two together. You have nice kinner and Anna's buwe could use a gut Amish man in their lives. They have gotten out of hand, I'm afraid, but with proper discipline, they could grow to become gut Amish men."

Anna returned to a quiet group. She looked around at all the sober expressions and fear ran through her. What had been said in the short time she'd left everyone?

"So, did you take Rachel's temperature?" Rose asked her daughter.

"Jah, it's only a hundred degrees. Not a real fever. Could be just from being outside, but I'm going to try to get her to rest and stay away from the other kinner, just in case."

"Gut idea," Beth said. "We were just having a nice chat, Anna. Don't look so *schlimm*."

"I don't mean to look sad, but you all look so serious. Did I miss something?"

Abe cleared his throat. "Your family is just concerned for you. They have reservations about our future."

"Well, I hope you know Abe and I are mature adults. We certainly won't marry if it's not the right thing to do. So you can all stop worrying!" Anna placed her hands on her hips, daring anyone to speak. Goodness, she never let her temper get the best of her like this. Nerves can really affect you!

"Sorry," Beth responded. "Of course we're concerned. Everything is happening so quickly. Maybe you should slow down a wee bit."

"And maybe you should stay out of it! Look at the mess you've made of your own life."

"Beth! Anna! Stop right now." Isaiah put his hands in the air, motioning for silence.

Abe ran his hand through his hair. "It seems everyone is on edge. Maybe we should leave tomorrow."

Anna burst into tears and ran from the room.

"Now look what you've done," Rose said, turning to Beth.

Isaiah stood and walked to the window above the sink. "Let's all take a deep breath. Abe, it would not be wise to leave under a cloud. Anna is very emotional right now. I think she's scared and has guilt about this whole thing, but she needs to move forward in her life—just as you do. We'll keep an eye on the kinner. I think you and Anna should take a nice long walk by yourselves and try to relax. This is not an easy situation."

Abe nodded. "Denki. Jah, I think you're right. We need to express our feelings to each other. I've been on edge myself. I want so badly for everything to be perfect, but that's not realistic. Of course, there will be problems when you put two families together who've suffered as much as ours have."

He turned to Beth. "Would you go ask Anna if she'd take a walk with me?"

"Why don't you go ask her yourself?"

"Beth!" Rose sent darts her way.

"What did I say now? It's not that I don't want to, but I think it would be better if Abe went himself. Anna's so upset."

Abe stood, nodding. "Jah. So where did she go?"

"Probably upstairs to her room. I'll show you. Follow me."

Abe climbed the stairs behind Beth. She pointed out Anna's room and left. He knocked gently on the closed door.

"What?"

"It's me, Anna. May I come in?"

"I guess so."

He found her sitting on the edge of the bed with a wad of tissues in her hand. Her eyes were red and swollen.

"Anna, why are you so upset? Your family is concerned for you, that's all."

"They're ruining everything. I'm sorry I had them come by. Especially Beth. She never knows when to keep quiet."

"May I sit next to you?"

Anna moved closer to her pillow and patted the bed beside her as she nodded. He took a seat. "May I hold your hand?"

"If you want to." She sniffed and took a fresh tissue for her eyes.

"I do want to." He took her free hand in his and used his thumb to caress her fingers. "I want this to work, Anna. I really do, and I believe it can. We're both walking on glass this week-end. It's not easy meeting family and watching the kinner as they sort through their own feelings. We shouldn't expect things to go perfectly."

"But you want to leave already," she said, her voice cracking.

"I shouldn't have said that. I'm sorry. Of course we'll stay. When I think about you when I'm home in Ohio, I get a gut feeling in my heart. It feels right to care about you. I can't call it love—not yet, but it's a positive feeling. I pray a lot about you and Gott seems to give me courage to continue. Don't you feel it's okay?"

Anna nodded. "Jah. At first, I didn't. I guess I felt I was somehow betraying Jeremiah. But I want a real home again. You're the first man I've had any feelings for at all."

He squeezed her hand. "I feel the same towards you. I find you very lovely."

"Not so lovely when I yell at my schwester," she said, her forehead creased.

Abe laughed. "Every family has its moments. Beth loves you and is just concerned that if this doesn't work out, you'll be hurting again."

"She may be right. I'm scared, Abe."

He reached over and drew her close. She laid her arms around his back and kept her head on his shoulder. He was strong and had a masculine scent of the outdoors. It was not unpleasant. For a brief moment, she felt like a woman again. A woman who needed a relationship with a man. They stayed entwined for another minute and then she pulled away.

His eyes were tender. Jah, she could one day care for this man. Oh, that it wasn't an impossibility.

"Would you like to take a walk with me? You haven't shown me your whole farm."

"But the kinner—"

"Your family said they'd watch them."

"Then let's. We have a new kid. The nanny goat is so proud. And maybe we'll check for eggs." Anna felt hope again. There would be problems. Many. But with God in the mix, it could work.

Abe put his hand out for her and they walked together down the hallway to the stairs.

Chapter Thirteen

Saturday was busy for Josiah. Mostly lookers, but two people wanted him to come by to give estimates on doing over their kitchens. He finally found the time to work on his latest project, but without an employee, it was difficult to get much accomplished, especially on a week-end. He'd have to put an ad in the local paper for help. For some reason, he'd been reluctant.

Around five, he went into the showroom to close up for the day, when he saw a small Volkswagen pull into the parking area. He watched as a young woman climbed out the driver's side. Sure enough, it was Nicole from the library. He had almost forgotten her promise to research books in the Greek language for him. He held the door open for her as she approached.

What a sweet smile she gave. Too bad she wasn't Amish. She came in and dropped a large manila envelope on one of the counters, removed her woolen jacket and tossed it over a chair. "See? I didn't forget you. It just took me time to get everything together."

"I really appreciate it, Nicole. Denki, or should I say, thanks."

She giggled. "Either is the same. My father came from an Amish family, so I know some of the Deitsch."

"Huh. I didn't even suspect you had Amish blood in you. Why did he leave?"

"To marry my mother, I guess. He doesn't talk much about it."

"Does he still see his family?"

"Only one brother. Everyone else kind of ignores him."

"That must be painful."

"He never talks about it. So, anyway, do you want to see what I found?"

"I do, but first, can I get you anything to drink? Tea? Lemonade?"

"No, I'm fine. My mother will have dinner ready when I get home, so I don't want to spoil my appetite." She looked around at her surroundings. "This is nice, Josiah. Very professional looking. Were you closing? It's kind of dark in here."

"Actually, I was, but I have nowhere to go, so I'm glad you stopped by."

"Why don't you come home with me then? We always have extra food."

"Oh, I couldn't do that."

"Why not? Honest, it might be fun for dad to have someone to talk to about the old days."

"But your mother—"

She pulled an iPhone out of her purse and hit speed dial. Looking up at Josiah, she whispered. "I'll ask."

After a quick conversation, she hung up and smiled

at him. "See? We're having spaghetti and meatballs, so there's plenty of food. She wants you to come."

Josiah shook his head. "You're very persuasive. Spaghetti is one of my favorite dishes. I'll just lock up in the back."

"I'll drive you since it will be dark when you want to come back."

"That's too much trouble. I'll take my buggy."

"I insist. This whole thing was my idea, so let me do the driving."

"Well, if you put it that way. I should change my clothes first, though, if you don't mind waiting."

"No prob. I'll just look around at your sample cabinets. I'm still hoping to buy a table from you when I save enough money."

"I'll be right back." He went into his bedroom and changed into clean clothes after washing his face and upper torso. He shook his head over the tub to remove any loose wood chips or sawdust. Then he combed it in place and headed up front where he found Nicole reading about the different kinds of wood.

"You have to have a lot of knowledge to work with all these different kinds of woods. Did you go to a special school or train with someone?" she asked as they left the showroom. He locked the front door behind him.

As he climbed into the passenger seat he answered. "I worked with someone in Ohio before I came to Pennsylvania. I always loved working with my hands." He pulled the seat belt across his lap and clicked it in place.

"Well, you're very talented." She zipped along the roads, taking the corners at a high speed, causing Josiah to grab the door handle more than once.

She looked over and smiled. "Scared?"

"A little," he said, forcing a smile.

"Don't be. We're almost there." She pulled into the drive of a home he'd passed many times and admired. It was a two-story colonial built of stone.

"Nice place. Is it as old as it looks?" he asked as they climbed out at the same time.

"Over a hundred years, I think. It's cool in the summer, but unfortunately, cool in the winter as well. It's hard to heat."

"I know all about that."

When they came in the front door using her key, they heard her mother in the back of the house. "Hi, I'm in the kitchen."

After introductions were made, Nicole asked where her father was.

"He's showering. He'll be right down. Would you like a beer, Josiah?"

"No thanks. I'm not a drinker."

"So I see you're Amish. Nicole forgot to mention that."

"I didn't think it mattered."

"It doesn't. I hope you like spaghetti," she asked Josiah.

"Yes, ma'am. I like just about anything, and spaghetti is one of my favorites."

"Good. It will be ready in about half an hour. Nicole, show him the new entertainment room."

"I doubt he'd be interested," Nicole said.

"No, I'd like to see it," Josiah said enthusiastically. Since he'd just finished building cabinets for an English family for their entertainment room, he wanted to compare.

She took him into a separate wing of the house—an add-on—and turned up the dimmer lights. Instead of theatre-type seating, there were several matching sofas on various platforms so the huge screen was visible from every seat. Somehow the period-style furnishings blended with the modern large screen television and multiple speakers.

"My mother designed it."

"It's very cool. Does she decorate homes for a living?"

"Nope, just for fun. The sound system is amazing, but dad has a fit if I fool with it. I'll have to let him show you another time, if you're interested."

Was he? He wasn't quite sure. It felt almost as if he'd been transported to another planet. He'd never seen such a large screen television—even in stores.

"Want me to show you around the house?"

"Sure."

They went back into the main section and she took him through a long el-shaped room with a grand piano at the end and matching sofas on each side of a marble fireplace.

"Do you play the piano?" he asked, stroking the shiny ebony finish of the top.

"I'm not great, but I do play."

"Would you play something for me?"

She sat on the bench and looked up at him. "What do you like? Classical? Jazz? Country?"

"Goodness, can you do all that?"

She laughed. "No, but I thought I'd ask."

"Whatever you want to play." He stood back and folded his arms.

"Let me see. Okay. Here's a Bach fugue I like."

She played brilliantly. Josiah was totally amazed at her talent. When she finished, she sat back on the bench and looked up with a smile. "Like it?"

"Oh jah. Beautiful. Do you do concerts?"

She rose and led him away from the piano. "Goodness, no. I'm not that good. I just play for my own entertainment. My father plays the violin. Sometimes we do duets in our church."

"I'd love to hear you."

"So come to church with us sometime. We're playing late in March. I'm not sure of the date."

"That sounds like a long time away."

"I'm sure we'll see each other many times before the concert," she said touching his arm and motioning towards the hallway.

"Dinner's served," her mother called out. Her father was just coming down the stairs as they were walking past. Nicole stopped and introduced them. Her father grinned as he gave Josiah the one-pump handshake the Amish were known for. Josiah smiled back and greeted him in the Deitsch. "*Wie geht es*?"

"Fine, just fine. Come, we'll have dinner and talk. It's been a while since I spent time with an Amish man."

"Daddy, he's a local craftsman. You should see the cabinets he makes."

"Oh, you have the showroom up the road?"

"Jah. That's mine."

"I'll have to stop in sometime."

"Please do. Your daughter just showed me your interesting entertainment room."

"You like it?"

"Jah, it's beautiful. Very different."

"You can sit across from Nicole," her mother suggested as they walked into the dining area of the kitchen. "Sorry we're eating in here instead of the dining room, but I already had it set up."

"Kitchens are my favorite rooms," Josiah said, smiling over.

The food was served family style and there was enough food for ten people. He helped himself to a generous portion of pasta plus a meatball, and then passed it on.

"I didn't make salad tonight, but I stopped at the market and picked up a chocolate cake for dessert. Do you like chocolate, Josiah?" Nicole's mother asked.

"Jah. I love it!"

The meal went quickly. The father talked almost continually about his experiences as a boy growing up Amish. Nothing much had changed. Josiah could relate to all his stories.

"Then he met me," her mother said, cocking her head to the side as she looked over at her husband.

"I've never looked back—at least not with regrets," he said, smiling warmly at his wife.

"I'm glad it happened that way," Nicole said, grinning. "Or I wouldn't be here."

"Nor would I," Josiah said.

After dessert and coffee, Nicole drove Josiah back to his place. "Do you want me to come in for a while?" she asked, unexpectedly.

Josiah wasn't used to women being so forward and it alarmed him. This could be a bit dangerous. An Amish man and an English woman alone at their age?

"I… I guess another time," he said. "I'm pretty tired.

It's been quite a week. My assistant left me and I'm doing everything by myself now."

"Oh, too bad," she said.

He wasn't sure if he detected sorrow or annoyance in her tone. It couldn't be helped.

"I hope you find a replacement soon. Too bad I'm working at the library."

"Jah. So thanks for researching the books for me. I'll check it out the first chance I get. And thank your parents again for having me over for dinner. It was very delicious. Sure beats my bologna sandwich."

She smiled faintly and waited for him to get to the door before gunning the engine and heading for the street.

So it was anger. Josiah lit a lantern and sat down by the window, looking out at the star filled sky. Nicole was very pretty, friendly, came from a nice family, and definitely interested in pursuing some sort of relationship with him. But it didn't feel right. Not at all.

He visualized Beth and her modest ways. Yah, she had a strong personality, but she also had strong moral values. She would never have been that forward. It was so silent. He missed Beth more at that moment than he ever had before, but they couldn't reconcile. He was too hurt. If they ever did resume their friendship—and that's all it would be—it would have to be initiated by Beth. Chances of even that were slight indeed.

Chapter Fourteen

The rest of Abe's visit went fairly smoothly. Rachel followed John around constantly until Anna took her aside and suggested she leave the young man alone, since he was older and obviously just trying to be polite about her tagging along. Rachel immediately became teary-eyed, but spent the rest of the time playing with her dolls.

Zach and his children came to visit, leaving his wife, Lottie time to rest. He and Abe bonded quickly. Anna regretted the time taken from her, but she knew it was important to get the family in on this event. She leaned heavily on their opinions and this was such a major decision. It was a visiting Sunday rather than a preaching Sunday, so during the day, some of her cousins stopped by with their families. She barely saw Abe alone. Once they met in the kitchen when she was busy arranging meats on a platter with the other women. Abe came over to her to discuss the driver.

"He'll be here in an hour, Anna. Do you think we could spend a few minutes alone?"

"I was hoping to, jah. Maybe my cousin Mabel can handle things for a few minutes. We can go sit in the sewing room off the hallway for privacy."

Mabel agreed to be in charge. Anna led Abe to the small, bright, room used for sewing and quilting, and she closed the door behind them.

"How do you think it went?" she asked Abe, studying his expression.

His smile seemed forced, but he nodded. "Gut, considering there are so many people involved. If it was just you and me…"

"It would be simpler, that's for sure. I'm sorry about Rachel."

"Sorry? For what?"

"I'm afraid she hounded John. I finally had to talk to her about it."

"John's a gut kid. He thinks she's cute. I was just hoping he and Luke would hit it off better. Maybe in time."

"And when Allie comes around, my Rachel will have someone more her age and a maed at that."

"*If* she comes around." Abe took a seat by the sewing machine and Anna moved a side chair to be closer to him, and sat down.

"Do you want to keep trying?" she asked hesitantly.

He reached across and took one of her hands. "Jah. Definitely. Can you come next week-end? I can pay for your driver."

"Maybe it will work out to travel, though we're supposed to have a snowstorm later in the week."

"This is a bad time to make plans."

"Jah, but we can always cancel. I have enough money to pay for the driver, Abe. I don't want you to do that. I'm sure Dinah would be glad to have me there. Her house is small though. Maybe I should just bring Rachel this time."

"Nee, the buwe need more time together as well. They can stay with us. It would work out. We have extra room. Now." He looked down at her hand and then pulled his arm back.

She knew he was thinking about his wife and children who had died in the accident. Extra room. Grief never died.

"Maybe that will work," she said softly. They sat silently for a few moments.

"Denki for having us this week-end. It meant a lot of extra work for you."

"Abe, if this does work out and we do end up as one family, I'll be working like this every day. I don't consider it 'work' since I love being a wife and mudder. You have very nice kinner. I understand the older ones being less anxious to meld into one family. They've gotten used to things the way they are."

"Jah, it's really Allie I worry about the most, though it was fun to see how excited my buwe were when you were there baking their cakes and adding some fun and laughter. We've all missed that."

"I'm sure. Are they packed up or should I go check the bedrooms?" she asked.

"They're ready. I saw to that earlier. Benny doesn't want to go back. He's really enjoying your buwe."

She grinned over. "Jah, and Mark and Matthew love having him here."

They both stood and Anna shoved the chair back

to its original position. When she turned, Abe put his arms around her and held her gently. "I hope it works for us, Anna."

"Jah, me too." They stood a few minutes more resting in each other's arms. There was nothing more. No kiss. No words. But Anna knew they were drawing closer. It was scary. If it didn't work out with the kinner, there would be pain. Again. She prayed silently for everything to work out for them and then they left the room and she returned to the kitchen.

When the driver arrived, she and Matthew and Mark walked out to the car with Abe and his boys. Rachel's cold was worse and Anna didn't want her outside. The child was coughing more. Luke stayed in his room.

The children said goodbye first. John and Benny gave Anna a hug and then Abe nodded and gave her a great smile. "I'll call you next Thursday at one again to see if you're coming."

"If we get that storm, I probably won't be able to make it to the phone, Abe."

"Oh jah, I hadn't thought of that. Well, I'll try anyway. If I don't get an answer, I'll figure the trip is off due to the weather. And then I'll call the following Thursday. Okay?"

"Jah. Fine. I'll schedule a driver, just in case. I can always cancel if it doesn't work out."

"Are we going too?" Mark asked his mother as Abe climbed in the front seat.

"Jah, if you buwe behave yourselves."

"Golly, there's always a 'but'!"

Anna rested her hand on his shoulder and waved as

the driver turned towards the road. After the car was out of sight, they returned to the house.

Mark frowned as they removed their jackets. "I wish Benny could stay with us forever. He's nicer than Luke."

"Ach, not nice to say, Mark. Luke is just having a hard time right now. He'll be better soon."

"I think he's scared Benny's daed will be mean to him."

"That's ridiculous. Abe is a very kind man and would be a gut daed."

"Tell that to Luke."

"Maybe I will when we have a little quiet. Right now we have to go see our guests."

As Anna returned to the kitchen, she looked over at Rachel. Her face was flushed and her eyes glassy. She was sitting on the floor next to the kitchen fireplace holding one of her dolls. When Anna knelt down to feel her daughter's head, she was shocked. It was the hottest she'd ever felt it. "Honey, you have to get into bed. I need to take your temperature."

"Why?" Her hair was actually damp, a few straggling strands laid against her forehead.

"You're a sick maed. How do you feel?" she asked Rachel as she reached for her hand and led her towards the stairs.

"Stinky."

"Poor boppli. I'm sorry I didn't notice sooner." When they got to her room, she helped her daughter undress and before putting on a nightie, Anna wiped her sweating body with cool washcloths. Then she covered her with a sheet and went for the thermometer. She wished everyone would leave, but it was difficult to make that request of her family and friends, who were enjoying themselves.

Rachel's temperature was over a hundred and four. Anna's heart pounded as she read the results. "I'm going to get you some water and juice to drink, Rachel, and I'm going to ask our guests to leave."

Tears crept down the child's cheeks. "Am I gonna die, Mamm? Like Daed and Abe's kinner?"

"Oh, mercy, nee! You'll be fine in a couple days. You just have a flu or something, honey. But you need to rest and take care of yourself."

Anna leaned over and kissed her daughter on her flushed cheek. She wiped away the tears and removed Rachel's kapp. Then she untwisted the braid and allowed her child's hair to be free. "You'll be more comfortable this way," she said.

"Mamm, will you come right back? I'm scared to be alone."

"Sure. I'll be gone only a couple minutes. I'll put the cot in your room tonight so I can be right alongside of you. How does that sound?"

"Gut. You won't let anything bad happen to me?"

"Nee, my *liebschdi*."

When she got downstairs, she discovered most of her friends had already left. She told her boys about Rachel's fever. "So you're going to have to obey without fuss. Your schwester is real sick and I'll be busy taking care of her."

They looked concerned. Matthew nodded. "I'm worn out from everything anyway. I'm gonna relax. How about you, Mark? Wanna play a game?"

"I guess. Where's Luke?"

"Still upstairs," Matthew answered. "Mamm, tell him we need him when you go back up."

"All right. I have to get juice for Rachel."

"Will she get better?" Mark asked, his brows furrowed.

"Of course, but if she's still real sick tomorrow, I'll have to take her to the doctor."

"Can we go, too?" Matthew asked.

"We'll see. Actually Aenti Beth is coming over tomorrow morning. Maybe I'll just leave her in charge and take Rachel myself. Hopefully, we won't have to take her."

"I thought she was pretty quiet all day," Mark said.

Anna took a pitcher with juice and a tall plastic glass with a bendable straw up the stairs. She stopped long enough at Luke's door to tell him the boys wanted him to join them for a game. He seemed pleased and said he'd go down to join them.

Rachel had fallen asleep. A feeling of fear nearly overwhelmed Anna as she studied her daughter's slight frame pressed against the sheet. *Oh, Lord in heaven, make my little one well. Bitte.*

She would give anything to have her Jeremiah back with her right now. He'd know what to do. She touched her daughter's cheek lightly to judge the fever. It was too soon to expect a change, and there was none.

Next week-end would be out of the question. Even though it was days away, she wouldn't take Rachel out in the cold so soon after being this sick. Maybe they should wait for spring to see each other again. That thought was quickly dismissed. No, if there was to be a wedding, probably the sooner the better. The longer they waited, the more difficult it might be for the older ones to accept change in their lives.

Well, no point even thinking about it. Rachel was her priority. She nudged her gently to begin the liquids. Dehydration could set in quickly with a small person. She'd found that out when Luke was two. They almost lost him, due to his being dehydrated from a throw-up bug. He'd ended up in the hospital overnight. What a nightmare.

Later, when she set up the cot next to her daughter, Anna set her wind-up alarm to go off in two hours. She planned to force liquids down every two hours.

Abe waited until they got into their home before sitting down with the boys to discuss the week-end. He made them sandwiches when they got back and his sister, Naomi, had left half a shoofly pie for them, which they devoured in minutes.

Before they started to clear the table, he motioned for them to sit. "How do you like Anna's kinner?" he asked them.

"Great!" Benny said, grinning. "She's got cool sohns."

Abe turned towards John. "Well?"

He shrugged. "Okay, I guess. Rachel's cute."

"She took a fancy to you," Abe said with a smile. "Anna was afraid she was annoying you."

"She was, a little."

"I think she'll really like Allie, Daed," Benny said.

"That's what I'm hoping."

"Are you really gonna get married?" John asked, his voice cracking slightly.

"It depends."

"On?"

"Lots of things. First of all, Allie has to like Anna enough to accept her."

"As a mudder? You think that can really happen?" John asked, his mouth firm.

"Look, buwe. No one will ever really take the place of your mudder, but we have to face the fact that she is gone. She will never be back. Do you think Allie should stay with your aenti forever? Don't you think she'd be better off being raised with a mudder figure and with her bruders and her daed?"

John looked down at the table and folded his arms. "I guess if you put it that way."

"Jah, you're being selfish," Benny said, glaring over at his brother.

"That's not nice, Ben," Abe said to his younger son. "John just has reservations, is all."

"Jah, it's not selfish to think about things, Ben." John put his hands on the table and leaned forward glaring back.

Benny spoke up. "But I'd like Anna to take care of me. She's a nice lady. Okay, she's not our real mamm, but she sure makes gut cakes and she smiles all the time."

"That's only because she wants everyone to like her," John said sternly.

"There's nothing wrong with that," his father said. "We could stand seeing some smiles come from you once in a while, sohn."

John's mouth dropped open. "Don't I smile?"

"Not often," Abe said quietly.

"Hardly ever," Benny added. "You always look sad."

"Maybe 'cause I am."

"Oh, John," Abe said, reaching across the table to touch his son's hand. "I'm sorry it's been so hard on you. I've been so wrapped up in my own grief, that maybe I haven't been there for you the way I should."

"Nee, Daed. You were gut. I know you've done your best. I just miss Mamm so much sometimes." He put his hands over his face and began to weep.

Benny looked shocked to see his brother so upset and began to cry himself.

Abe extended his arms. "Come here, buwe. Let me hold you both."

They went over and knelt on the floor beside their father as he enveloped them in his arms. "Gott, please help us through this. We can't do it alone."

And Abe wept.

Chapter Fifteen

Beth let herself in Anna's kitchen door the next morning, surprised not to be met by her sister. The boys were eating dry cereal and arguing about passing the sugar bowl when she came through the utility room.

"Where's your mudder?" she asked as she removed her woolen jacket.

"Sleeping," Luke answered as he pushed the sugar towards Matthew, causing some to spill.

"At this hour?"

"Rachel's sick and Mamm was up all night with her. She came down to tell us before," Luke told her.

"Oh my, what a shame. What's wrong with your schwester?"

Luke shrugged. "I don't know, but Mamm wants to take her to the doctor's when you arrive."

"I'll go right up then."

When Beth got to Rachel's room she heard Anna talking softly to her daughter. She knocked on the door and Anna told her to come in.

"Oh, Beth, I'm glad you're here. Rachel coughed most of the night. I have to get her to the doctor right away."

Beth felt her niece's forehead. "She's pretty warm."

Rachel opened her eyes and stared at her aenti. "I feel awful," she managed to say.

"Poor little maed. I'm sorry. We'll get you right to the doctor's. Daed put a heater in the buggy for me. It should still be warm. Do you want to take my buggy, Anna, and I'll stay home with the buwe?"

"Jah, gut idea. Can you walk, Rachel, if I hold your arm?" Anna asked.

"Sure. But when I went to the bathroom before I felt weird. Like all dizzy."

"We'll support you, Rachel. Come on." Beth moved to the side of the bed and she and Anna took sides and helped her to her feet.

"I'm okay." Rachel giggled softly. "I feel funny— like a boppli."

After they dressed her and twisted her hair under her kapp, they placed her into the back of the buggy and covered her with old quilts.

"Are you taking her to Dr. Hudson?"

"Jah, he should be in. It's Monday."

"I wish we had phones. I'll be on pins and needles till you get back."

"I know. If an emergency arrives, I'll call Donna Jenkins, across the street. I always carry their number with me. She could send her son over to get you. But I'll only do that if I have to."

"All right. Get going."

Rachel continued coughing the whole trip to the doctor's which took about half an hour. Fortunately, there were only two patients ahead of them. Anna held Rachel in her arms as the child dozed between coughing episodes.

When Dr. Hudson examined her, he used his stethoscope on her back as well as her front. He took longer than usual, pressing her little rib cage gently. His face remained expressionless. Finally, after writing on her chart, he turned toward Anna.

"Your daughter has bronchitis. A pretty bad case, Anna. I'm afraid we'll have to admit her."

Anna was standing when he spoke with her and she reached for the back of a chair to steady herself. "The hospital?" She glanced over at Rachel, who was staring at her, fear pouring from her eyes.

"Oh, it's okay, honey. The doctor just wants to be sure we take gut care of you, right, Dr. Hudson?"

"Absolutely. You're a very special young lady," he said, realizing how frightened Rachel had become. "We want to give you medicine and lots of good food to make you better. You won't be there long, honey."

"I don't want to go there. I want to go home," she cried out between coughs.

Anna put her arms around her. "Nee, you have to do as the doctor says, Rachel, but I'll stay with you. Aenti Beth can take care of your bruders."

"You won't leave me even for a minute?"

Anna tried to smile. "Only to go to the bathroom once in a while. Okay?"

Rachel nodded, but clutched her mother for dear life.

"I need to make some calls, Anna, before she's admitted," the doctor said. "You can stay in here and I'll phone from the other room."

After he left, Anna helped her daughter get down from the examining table and she took her in her arms and gently rocked back and forth. "Try to sleep a little. You were awake most of the night." The child nodded and burrowed her head into her mother's apron top. "I'm glad you're my mudder."

"Well, I'm real glad you're my dochder," Anna said as she held back tears.

Two hours later, Rachel was in a hospital bed in Lancaster. They had gone by ambulance without turning on the sirens. Anna sat in the front with the driver. Somehow she'd have to get word to her brother to fetch the horse and buggy left behind. So many difficulties when you don't own a phone. Once they got to the hospital, Anna called her neighbor, who sent her son across to tell Beth and the boys, who in turn, sent Luke to his Uncle Zach's to inform him of the buggy and his niece being admitted to the hospital.

Zach, on his way to retrieve the buggy, stopped at a friend's place where their elder son hopped in so that he could drive Zach's buggy back while Zach took care of Beth's buggy, which Anna had borrowed—

Goodness! It took a lot of coordinating, but somehow everything eventually worked out and Anna was free to remain at the hospital with her daughter.

Rachel received attention from everyone on the floor. The nurses were wonderful, as well as the aids, the doctors—even the dietician who made sure she talked to Anna about Rachel's likes and dislikes, though at this point she was strictly on IV's and liquids. They did allow sherbet, which Rachel devoured quickly—between spells of coughing.

She was given x-rays and then a therapist came by to work on the congestion. Anna knew her daughter was getting excellent care and she was extremely grateful, but fear kept creeping in. She knew her parents would arrive soon, once they were able to leave the farm. It would be helpful to have them with her at this time, but she found herself thinking of Abe. She wished he could be there for support. Of course, that was out of the question.

Anna wrote a quick note to her friend in Ohio. Dinah would want to know about Rachel. She needed prayer from other believers. After scribbling a short message on scrap paper, she asked a nurse's aide for an envelope. One of the other aids even purchased a stamp for her and took the letter to be mailed. Anna was grateful for the young girl's concern.

Rachel slept between visits from the nursing staff and when her cough allowed. The child looked so frail in the sterile white bed, hooked up to an IV and beeping monitors. Anytime she awoke, the first thing she did was look over at Anna to make sure she was nearby. Once while Rachel slept, Anna left long enough to use the lady's room and pick up a Danish from a snack bar. When she returned to the room, Rachel was being comforted by a nurse. Her tears nearly broke Anna's heart. She had to remain strong for her daughter. Not an easy task.

Rose and Isaiah showed up around six and it gave Anna a chance to eat something more substantial in the cafeteria. Rose sat and held Rachel's hand the entire time Anna was gone. Isaiah paced in the hallway, tugging on his beard. Concern showed from every cell of his lean body.

There was little improvement. Somehow Anna caught enough sleep that first night to function the next day. Her parents returned around noon with a note from Beth, sending her support and love to both Anna and Rachel. They also brought Rachel's giraffe, which Anna had purchased in Ohio, and the child clutched it—releasing it only when the doctor came to examine her.

After his examination, the doctor walked into the hall with Anna behind him. He turned and spoke softly. "The antibiotics haven't kicked in yet. We can't release her until she shows definite improvement. In fact, Anna, she'll probably have to remain here the rest of the week."

She nodded. "I understand." She put her hands over her face and whispered the unthinkable. "Will she get well?"

She felt his hand on her arm. "Anna, she's very sick, but we're doing everything possible to make her well again. Though I can't promise, I believe she'll be fine. It just may take a little longer than we'd like. I'm going to order another chest X-ray. They can bring it to the bedside. We have to watch that it doesn't develop into pneumonia."

"I see."

"I'll check on her every chance I get. I'll be in the hospital all day."

"And tomorrow?"

"Yes, I'm on all week. The staff knows how to reach me at all times."

"Denki."

He squeezed her arm and moved off to another room. She stood and stared straight ahead. This had turned into a nightmare. What started off as a simple cold…should she have foreseen this? Was she a bad mother to have allowed her to play in the snow with a cold? Was it her fault the child was in the hospital— fighting for her very life?

She heard Rachel call her. This was no time for re- flection or self-battering. Her daughter needed her by her side. Anna stood straight, wiped her tears on her sleeve and went back to Rachel's bedside.

Chapter Sixteen

Josiah ordered three Greek books through the mail. It would be slower than using a computer, the way Nicole had suggested, but he didn't want to be beholden to her or anyone else. After placing the letter in the mailbox and flagging it for the mailman, he made his way into the workroom and began his day's work. Around nine, he placed the open sign in the window and unlocked the front door. Before he had a chance to return to the workshop, he saw Nicole's car pulling off the main road and into his parking lot.

He wished he'd never met the girl. He didn't need an English woman in his life—now or ever.

She came through the door carrying a small grocery bag. "Hi, look what I brought. Did you start your coffee yet?" she asked as she removed a plaid scarf from her head and took off her jacket, placing it over a chair.

"Nee. I don't usually have coffee until I've worked an hour or two."

"Everyone needs coffee," she mused. "I'll make it. Show me where you keep everything."

"That's okay. Really."

"Josiah, I only have an hour before I need to be at the library. Let me make the coffee! I brought goodies from the bakery."

Feeling totally at her mercy, he led her into the private area and pointed out the coffeepot which hadn't been cleaned since the day before. She clicked her tongue at him and rinsed it out before asking for fresh grinds. He opened the cupboard and handed the can over. "Just make enough for six cups."

"Sure, whatever." She began humming a tune as she measured the grinds into the strainer. He stood, arms folded, watching as she moved about his small work area as if she owned it. He didn't know whether to be annoyed or amused.

"Don't you want to see what I brought?" she asked, pointing to the counter where she had laid the bag.

"Sure." He walked over and opened it to discover four scones. "We can't eat all that," he said.

"Wow! You sound so excited," she said sarcastically. "I didn't know what to get."

"Oh, I like scones. I'm sorry I sounded ungrateful."

"It's okay. I know from living with my father, that most men don't have the greatest record for saying the right thing."

He laughed and then reached in the cabinet next to the sink for plates and mugs.

She looked at his choice of mugs. "Ugly. Don't you have something brighter?"

"Maybe. Let me look." He found a yellow mug. "Is this better?"

"Better than plain old everyday white. So, do you want me to order any books for you? Have you had a chance to go through my notes?"

"Oh jah, that was real nice of you. See? I remember my manners now." He chuckled as he reached for paper napkins and placed them on the small table next to the sink.

"I already sent my order in. It's in the mailbox as we speak."

"I told you I could order them on line and save you time."

"I don't mind waiting a couple more days. I didn't want to be a bother."

"Josiah, you aren't a bother. I like you. I think you must know that."

The back of his neck heated up and he feared it would be visible. "Jah well. That's nice of you to say."

"And I assume the feeling is mutual?" she tilted her head coyly and gave him a smile which brought the word "seductive" to his mind. This was getting out of hand. After all, he was a man with normal hormones and thoughts. It was time to put an end—

She sat on a chair and placed her legs up on an empty chair across from hers. Her jeans were way too tight. He avoided looking at her and spent time rinsing a glass, which was already clean.

"Why don't you sit with me while we wait for the coffee and tell me all about your projects for this week?"

Maybe he'd misread her. Perhaps she was just a friendly kind of girl. He sat down and cleared his throat.

"Well, I'm still working on a big kitchen. I hope to

finish it this week, at least the part I have to do here in the shop. Then I'll head over to the house and install it."

"Who's going to watch your shop for you?"

Uh oh. Was she hinting at working for him? That would never do. "I have friends. Not to worry."

"Oh, I wasn't worried." She looked over as the percolator brewed away. "I hate my job at the library. It's so boring. Maybe you can hire me."

"I... I need someone who knows the business."

"Really? You don't think you could teach me? I'm pretty quick to learn and I don't expect to be paid much."

"That's real nice of you to offer. I'll let you know if I need you."

"Mmm." She ran her tongue over her lower lip and took her napkin and folded it into a small square. "You should get one of those new coffee makers—the kind that brews one cup at a time."

"I don't have electricity."

"You have a generator. I see it."

"That's only for the refrigerator."

"So if you use it for one, you—"

"Nicole, I'm aware of what I can do."

"Sorry." Her mouth turned down and she stood up and walked over to the pot and turned off the gas. "Even if it's weak, I'd better pour mine now. I don't want to be late."

He knew he had offended her, but it couldn't be helped. He had a knack for saying the wrong thing to women sometimes. Maybe that's why his relationships never lasted.

"It looks pretty gut. I'll pour mine now too."

"I'll do it. Sit."

That's what he said to his dog when he lived at home. If she thought he was going to fall for her, she had another think coming. After all, it wasn't enough to be pretty and available, he was looking for something a lot more permanent.

They sat silently sipping the weak brew and picking at their scones. She let out a long sigh. "So have you ever been in love?" she asked out of the blue.

"That's a strange thing to ask a man."

"Is it? Why? I'll tell you about my past. I've been in love tons of times."

"That doesn't sound very gut."

"I guess it doesn't. I don't mean it was serious each time. Sometimes the guys didn't even know I was alive."

He laughed. "Goodness that must have been disheartening."

"I was a kid. My last real relationship was about a year ago. I thought I might even marry the guy, but it wasn't meant to be."

Josiah nodded and tore off another small piece of scone.

"Don't you want to know what happened?"

"Nicole, I think I'd better talk truth to you now before we go any further. I'm at a marriageable age. I'm Amish. I'll remain Amish. I have no interest in pursuing anything beyond friendship with you or anyone else who isn't Amish."

"You certainly know how to hurt a girl."

"We barely know each other."

"But I thought there was a strong feeling between us."

"I'm afraid you imagined it."

"I don't think so, but if you want to believe that, you can."

"Nicole, I'm in love with an Amish girl."

Her eyes darted. "Why didn't you tell me? You never said a word."

"It's not really your business, but the truth is, she doesn't love me."

"So why hang on? That's ridiculous!"

"Why? I can't even answer that, but all I know is, I can't get her out of my mind and hopefully someday we will be together."

"Wishful thinking. It's stupid."

"I don't appreciate that."

She rose abruptly, dumped the remaining coffee in his sink and headed to the front.

"Wait, don't go off mad, Nicole."

She turned as she reached for the outside door handle. "Don't worry about me being a pest. You won't see me again!" She slammed the door behind her and stomped over towards the car.

Josiah took a deep breath and let it out slowly. *Gut. That's over. Now maybe I can get some work done.*

He went back to the kitchen and moved the pot off the burner. Then he took out the last scone and gobbled it down, before returning to his project. He was pleased with himself. He had averted a difficult situation. Some men might think he was crazy, but he knew better. "Gott is pleased," he said aloud.

Chapter Seventeen

Beth watched through the window as Anna's three boys played in the fresh snow. About three inches had fallen during the night and it was a relief to get the boys out of the house. The board games weren't enough for three energetic kids. A buggy turned down their drive as she stood gazing at the front trees adorned in the layer of white flakes.

She couldn't make out who the visitor was at first, but then noticed it was her Aunt Ellie. When she got to the door, Beth took her shawl and invited her to sit.

"Actually, I'm here to watch Anna's buwe," Ellie said. "We just heard about Rachel. I'm sure you could use some help."

"Oh, could I. Denki, Aenti. Actually the buwe haven't been so bad, but I really want to get to the hospital to be with Anna and Rachel. It's hard without a phone. I have to wait for my parents to stop by each night to get a report. Apparently, Rachel isn't doing so gut."

Ellie patted her arm. "The gut Lord will watch over her."

"Jah."

"So can you get a driver? The roads are a little slippery and it would take you too long to get there by buggy."

"Yah, I don't like using the buggy in Lancaster. Too much traffic. I'll go across the street and see if I can use their phone to call Ted. He's usually available."

"I brought some left-over chicken pot pie. I made way too much."

"Gut. I hadn't even thought about dinner yet."

Things worked out, and Ted Darby came for Beth. As they came near Josiah's shop, she asked him to turn in. She'd had no plans to stop, but she felt compelled to tell him about Rachel.

When Josiah heard the bell from the front door, he peeked into the showroom and spotted Beth closing the door behind her. His heart jumped at the sight of her. He wiped his hands and went right over to her. "Beth, it's gut to see you."

"Jah." She appeared nervous as she twisted her bonnet ribbons as she spoke. "I wanted you to know about Rachel." As she told him about the child being in the hospital and her condition, his eyes softened.

"I'm so sorry. Poor Anna. She must be a wreck."

"We all are. She's got to get better…oh, Josiah." She put her head down and for the first time since the child became ill, Beth wept.

She felt his arms surround her and she relaxed her body against his, drawing strength. "It's so upsetting," she was able to add.

"Of course. Your family's been through so much. We must pray for her to get all better quickly."

"Jah, I guess that's why I'm here."

He moved away slightly and prayed for the child's health. When he finished, Beth moved apart.

"Denki. I have to go now. My driver is waiting."

"Can I do anything to help? Do you want me to go watch her buwe?"

"Nee, my aenti is there now. Zach's wife can't sit for them because she's having trouble with her pregnancy."

"I'm sorry to hear that. Please give Anna my love."

"I will."

"Can you stop by on your way home to let me know how Rachel's doing?"

"I'll try. It depends on the time."

"Of course. I'll continue to pray for all your family."

She nodded as she pulled her shawl closer, and left.

Josiah went in the back and knelt to pray. Everything else seemed insignificant when a child's life lay in the balance.

Abe and his brother-in-law, William, worked together on repairing Abe's thresher. John stood and watched as the men straightened the bent metal. When they were done, the three of them went in the house where Naomi was hanging clothes in the basement. Her five children were playing with Benny and Allie in the main living room area. They were building an extensive farmhouse with a large barn and multiple buildings out of blocks and Legos. It was quite a production and had to be rebuilt more than once as Allie and Becky, who was only over a year old formed the demolition committee.

After Naomi finished with the wash, the adults sat in the kitchen drinking hot tea. They heard a buggy on the drive.

"Expecting anyone?" William asked Abe.

"Nee, but you never know who's gonna show up."

"I'll check. You fellows must be tired," Naomi said, rising. "You worked out in the barn over three hours."

"Was it that long?" William asked as Naomi went to open the front door.

"So you and Anna are hitting it off pretty gut," William mentioned as he sipped his coffee.

"Jah. She's a very nice lady."

"And the kids?"

"They're gut kids. Just been through a lot is all."

"Do they respect you?"

"Too soon to say."

Abe looked up as Naomi walked in with their friend Dinah Stutzman. Their expressions spoke of trouble.

Abe stood and pointed to his chair. "Sit, Dinah. You look all upset."

"I just got a letter from Anna. Rachel's in the hospital."

Abe's mouth dropped open. He shook his head. "We were there a couple days ago. What on earth happened?"

"Apparently she has bronchitis real bad. They're worried about her. Poor Anna. She just wanted me to know so I could be praying."

"I wonder why she didn't write to me," Abe said.

"She mentioned you and said to try to get word to you so you can pray, too. She didn't know your address."

"Oh my," Abe said. "I have to go to her. She should have someone with her."

"Bruder, she has family there. Her parents, a schwester, her—"

"I feel she needs a man beside her. With her husband gone, I think I should be there."

He turned to his sister, eyes questioning.

"Jah, go. I'll take care of the kinner. You're right, this is a time to be with her and show her you care. And you obviously do."

"Jah, more than I realized. I need to get hold of a driver. I can walk down to Tom's place. It would be faster than hitching up the buggy."

"I'll drop you off, Abe," Dinah said. "I have to get back to the house. Hannah will need a feeding soon."

"Let me throw a few things in a toot and I'll tell the kids."

The children seemed concerned. Especially John. "Daed, tell Rachel I want to play checkers again, and she'd better get well real quick-like."

Abe patted his head. "I'll tell her, Sohn. Take care of your bruders while I'm gone."

John nodded.

Benny had tears in his eyes. "She won't die, will she Daed?"

Abe shook his head. "Nee. I'm sure she'll be just fine. Try not to worry."

"I'm gonna say a prayer right now." The child lowered his head and sat silently for several minutes as the others became quiet as well. Only Allie and her cousin, Becky, seemed untouched by the news and continued to knock apart the well-placed blocks. No one seemed upset about it. They just quietly rebuilt their buildings.

Tom was free to drive and asked for twenty minutes while he packed himself and Abe a bag of fruit and energy bars. Then his wife gave them bottles of spring water and they took off.

When Abe wasn't in prayer, he was thinking about Anna and what she was going through. The poor woman had been through so much already. Surely the Lord wouldn't take her sweet Rachel—the apple of her eye.

Chapter Eighteen

Anna watched as the nurse's aide took Rachel's temperature with the ear monitor. "It's down a little," she said as she smiled over at Anna, who grasped at any indication of improvement.

"How high is it?" she asked the girl.

"Just over one hundred and two. Still high, but at least it's coming down."

Anna nodded and stroked her daughter's arm. Her parents had just left for the night. They'd been so concerned. If only she could get word to them about the slight drop in Rachel's temperature. Sometimes the bishop would allow cell-phones when there was a situation like hers. She should ask her father to check the next time he came by. It would simplify things ever so much.

The doctor had seemed more optimistic this afternoon and said if she continued this way, he could let her eat a little more. Rachel never complained about being hungry. In fact, the child never complained—period.

She was such a dear. Anna smiled over at the sleeping child. Her cough was improving though the therapist still came in twice a day. Rachel cried when she saw them coming in with the breathing contraption, but she did as she was told. Mr. Giraffe was her constant companion. "He doesn't like me to cry, Mamm. So I'm brave when they make me breathe through that funny thing." Anna was so proud of the way she handled everything. A very brave little girl.

The staff thinned out in the evening and the floor became quieter as visitors left and the young patients were prepared for bed. Rachel was alone in her room since she was infectious, but there were other children even younger in other rooms and often there'd be several children crying at one time. At the moment all was quiet and Anna moved to the recliner and rested her head. She'd had so little sleep since Sunday, she was beyond exhaustion. The stress made her even more worn out. Maybe she could snatch a few minutes of sleep.

Anna had no idea how much time had passed when she felt a hand on her shoulder. She jumped slightly at the touch and rubbed her eyes as she looked up. It couldn't be! Surely she was dreaming! "Abe! Is it really you?"

"Jah, I just found out about Rachel. Dinah came by to tell me."

Anna stood up and extended her arms. Abe squeezed her tightly and kissed the side of her head. "Poor lovely Anna. I've been so worried about you. Have you had any rest?"

"Nee, not much."

"And Rachel—how is the little maed?"

"Her fever has dropped a wee bit. That's the first gut sign we've seen. The doctor was in a while ago and he seems more optimistic."

"Thank Gott."

He looked down at the sleeping child. "She looks like a little angel."

"Jah, she does," Anna said, following his gaze. "She is my little angel. I've been so sick over this."

"Of course." He reached for her hand, but she placed her arms around his waist again. "It is so gut to have you here, Abe. You can't believe how much I wanted you near me."

He nodded and held her tightly. "When I heard about Rachel, I just had to be with you. I realize now how much I care for you, Anna."

"And I, you. I knew if you were with me, I'd get through it. How long can you stay? Who's with the kinner?" She pulled back to hear his response.

"I'll stay as long as you need me. Naomi has the kids."

"She's such a dear. You really can stay for a while?"

"Jah. Between her and William they'll manage. If I could get word to Sam, he'd probably be more than willing to come and help them out. This time of year, things are slower on the farm, as you know."

"True."

They heard a small voice. Rachel was awake, staring at them. "Hi," she said, a smile creeping along her cheeks.

"Hi, little one. What's the idea of getting sick on us?"

"I didn't mean to."

"Nee, I'm sure you didn't. How do you like your giraffe? Your mamm said she wanted to buy you one."

"He's very nice. He's sad that I'm sick."

"Just like we are. But you're going to get all better real soon."

"Jah, that's what Mr. Giraffe told me, too."

Abe smiled and turned to Anna. "She looks pretty gut, considering."

"You should have seen her yesterday. Jah, now that her fever is going down a little, I think her eyes seem a bit brighter."

"My chest doesn't hurt as much, Mamm."

"You're not coughing as much, that's why. All those treatments are starting to work, honey."

"Yup. That's what they told me. They said if I was gut and did what they said, I'd get better faster. I'm awful tired though."

"Go back to sleep, Rachel. I'm going to go get some food with Abe. We'll be back real soon. Is that okay?"

"Jah. Denki for coming to see me, Abe."

"That's all right, honey. I was real worried about you and your mamm. The kinner said to say hi, and John told me to tell you he wants to challenge you to Checkers again."

Rachel grinned. "Tell him I'd like that, but he better learn more fancy moves, 'cause I'm gonna beat him next time."

They headed towards the hallway. On the way down in the elevator, Abe looked over at Anna and smiled. "It must be quite a relief to see her smile."

"You have no idea." The elevator stopped and they walked over to the cafeteria. After they each picked out a light meal, they sat at a window table.

"You look gut, Abe. How are the kinner?"

"They're fine. They talk a lot about you and your kinner. Benny wants to live with you." He grinned over.

"Hopefully, John will feel that way someday."

"It's a long trip back and forth, Anna. I think we should try to make up our minds soon, don't you? First, of course, we have to get Rachel all better, but on my way here, I was thinking about this whole situation and I came to the conclusion that we can't let a three-and-a-half year old child make the decision for two families. I believe in my heart that we are right for each other and in time, I think Allie will come to love you. How could she not?"

They were practically alone in the cafeteria. No one was faced their way, so he reached across the table to hold her hand. "What do you think?"

She nodded and smiled over. "I didn't think of it that way, but you're right. We, as adults, should make the decision based on our feelings and our judgement. In the end, it's better for her to have a mudder and be with you and her bruders than to continue where she is. You know I will love her as my own. I've always loved kinner."

"And you'd still want more of your own?"

She glanced down at her plate and nodded. "In time."

"Jah, in time. I understand. I feel the same. We also need to discuss where we'd live, Anna."

"I know. I've run it through my mind a dozen times. I can't imagine being so far from my family, but my farm isn't as large as yours and you have the livestock and of course you have your own family. So though it would be difficult, I'm prepared to leave Pennsylvania and make my home with you in Ohio, if that's what you want."

He squeezed her hand. "Anna, that makes it so much easier for me and the kinner, but I hate putting you through the pain of moving away from your loved ones."

"What choice do we have? One of us has to move."

He nodded. "I suppose when you look at all the factors, it would make more sense to settle in Ohio."

"At least I have Dinah there and I really like your schwester, Naomi, a lot. The other thing is Allie. I don't think it would be fair to take her away from everything that is familiar to the child. Especially from Naomi. It could be too traumatic for the little maed."

"You're a wonderful-gut woman, Anna. I believe I'm falling in love with you."

She bit her lip. "Denki." She looked down and pushed some potato chips to the side. She didn't know how to respond to his last words. They were very special and lifted her heart, but could she say them back?

"I think we should go back to Rachel soon," she said instead.

He smiled. "Jah. I'm not expecting you to say anything in return, Anna. Really. The fact you're willing to become my wife and take on my family is enough for me. I'll be eternally grateful."

They stayed at the hospital all night, dozing occasionally in the waiting room or the recliner, as they took turns being with Rachel. For the first time since she became sick, Rachel slept most of the night. Her cough was declining in intensity and frequency.

The next morning, the doctor came by early and was delighted to report her temperature was normal. "I'd like to watch her one more day, but if her fever doesn't return and her bronchial tubes sound as clear as I expect them to, she could go home tomorrow afternoon."

"Oh, that would be wonderful," Anna said. Abe nodded in agreement. Anna noticed the doctor was looking at Abe, waiting for an introduction.

Abe put his hand out and said, "I'm Anna's future husband."

Dr. Hudson beamed at them. "Well, isn't that nice. I'm happy for you Anna."

He turned to Abe, "And you are a fortunate young man. I've known Anna since she was a child, and they don't come any better."

"Jah, I'm finding that out," Abe said grinning.

"And she comes with a pretty nice family."

"Jah, I know that, too," Abe said, nodding in agreement.

After he left them, Abe asked if Anna was upset that he'd announced their decision to marry. "I don't know what came over me. I guess I wanted to shout it out to the world, but he was here instead."

Anna giggled. "It's fine. I'd have to tell him sooner or later anyway. I'll need to take all our records with me when I move. The only people I'm nervous about telling are my parents and Beth. We've always been so close."

"They'll all be welcome to visit anytime for as long as they want."

"Jah, that's nice. And hopefully they will come often. Maybe we should introduce Beth to your bruder."

"Sam?" Abe grinned. "I don't know if he'll ever settle down. He's different from me. I couldn't wait to have my own family. Sam runs scared."

"So does Beth. They'd have a lot in common, I guess."

Later in the day, Anna's parents came by to check on their grandchild. First, they were shocked to see Abe there. Rose looked pleased as Anna told how he heard about Rachel and how quickly he made it to her side. They were also excited to get the news of Rachel's improvement and possible discharge. "We'll wait till we hear from you tomorrow before heading back to the hospital then. Hopefully, she'll be home. Abe, you can stay with us if you want to."

"I'll just stay here at the hospital to keep Anna company," he said, smiling over at Anna.

"Jah, it helps to have you here," she said, nodding.

After her parents left, Rachel took a long nap. While she slept, Anna and Abe walked around the hospital to get some exercise. "Even though I'm exhausted, the relief gives me fresh energy," Anna said.

"True. It really helps to see that little one smiling again, that's for sure."

"Can you stay for a couple more days, Abe?"

"As long as you need me."

"Then I guess you're going to move in," she said, teasing. "Actually, I was hoping you might be there when I told them all about our plans. Especially the part about my moving to Ohio."

"Are you nervous about their reactions?"

"Jah, I guess a little. I know they want me to be happy again, it's just…"

"I know. It's not going to be easy. I'll stay, Anna, until you feel okay with my leaving."

"Denki. I could go for ice cream. What about you?"

"Just had the same idea. Let's stop and pick up ice cream cones and we'll get one for Rachel," he suggested.

"Oh, gut idea. I hope they have peanut butter ice cream. That's her all-time favorite."

Rachel was excited when they returned to her room. Her color was rosy and her head was cool. Anna was so grateful, she couldn't wipe the smile from her face.

Abe looked over and grinned at her. "You are sure a pretty lady."

Rachel nodded. "I'm the luckiest maed in the whole wide world. I have a pretty mamm who knows how to pick out giraffes and she's gonna marry a real nice man so I can have a dat again."

Anna's hand went to her heart. *Oh, denki, Gott.* Now for the rest of the family.

Around noon the next day, the doctor signed the release papers and Ted Darby was called to come for them. Anna wrapped her daughter in one of the quilts they'd brought her in, and Abe carried her to the waiting vehicle.

Rachel gabbed all the way home as Anna held her hand in the back seat. Abe turned around several times and nodded. Hopefully she'd be as happy when she found out they'd be moving. That would definitely be the difficult part of this whole situation. But their minds were made up now and only God could change the circumstances to alter their decision.

Chapter Nineteen

Anna made Rachel comfortable on the sofa so she could watch the others play. Her parents left for home shortly after they got in, since her father was concerned about his live stock. The boys behaved well and she wondered if it was because Abe was present. Or perhaps Rachel's illness had shocked them into better behavior. Whatever caused it, Anna was grateful.

"I wish I could play Monopoly," Rachel said, reticently, as she looked over at the others.

"We'll play with you," Luke said. "We just have to finish up our Parcheesi game first."

"Can I get you something to drink?" Anna asked her patient.

"Maybe later, Mamm." She smiled up at Abe and her mother as they stood by the sofa. "You guys can leave me alone now. I'm gut."

"Maybe we'll relax in the kitchen then," Anna said as she tucked the quilt under the sofa pillows. "You call me if you need anything."

When they sat down at the kitchen table, Abe covered an enormous yawn and shook his head. "I can't believe how tired I am. I don't know how you got through all this."

"Only with Gott's help. I'm almost afraid to try to sleep, I feel so wired up."

"My cousin doesn't know I'm here. I'd better leave soon so I won't shock him by arriving at night."

"Abe, why don't you stay next door with my bruder? Or you could go to my parents place. Mamm even mentioned it."

"I guess it would be better if I'm right next door. Think Zach would mind?"

"Of course not. He and Lottie would be glad to have you there. You might have to sleep on their sofa."

"At this point, the floor would feel gut."

"If you stay with the kinner, I'll go next door and check."

"Sure. Do you want one of your sohns to check for you?"

"Nee, that's all right. I know my bruder will be anxious to hear all about Rachel. I may be a couple minutes."

"Take your time. Maybe your kinner will let me play Monopoly with them. I'm quite the shrewd realtor."

She smiled as she reached for her shawl.

As she approached the backdoor, Anna heard a commotion. She peeked in the window and saw the younger children running around the kitchen with a rubber ball, giggling. No sign of her brother or Lottie. She let herself in and cornered her eldest nephew. "Where's your mudder?"

"Upstairs with Daed and some lady."

"Try to calm everyone down, Obie. It's awful noisy in here."

"I'll try."

Anna called upstairs and then saw her brother come out of his bedroom.

"Anna, how's Rachel?"

"Gut. We just brought her home. What's going on?"

"Lottie's in labor. Come on up. The mid-wife just arrived. That's gut news about Rachel."

"Oh mercy. Of all times for the boppli," Anna said under her breath. She took the steps two at a time and went right in to find her sister-in-law panting through a long contraction. Lottie looked over at her, but couldn't speak. Her eyes rolled back as she tried to deal with the pain. The mid-wife, Cindy, who had brought Anna's children into the world, looked over and smiled faintly. "Lottie's just about to deliver. Want to stay and help?"

"If you need me, sure."

Lottie stopped panting briefly and closed her eyes. "I feel another."

"You should start to feel like bearing down soon," Cindy said to her.

"Jah. Oh my."

Anna felt a pit in her stomach as she recalled her own deliveries. Lottie had been so fortunate with short labors and quick deliveries. Hopefully, this would be no exception.

Zach stood in the corner of the room, his eyes bulging out of his head. He was a worrier—each time. This was no exception.

Anna looked over at him. "It will be fine, Zach. Breathe easier."

"Oh jah. Sure."

Cindy leaned over the bed and reached under the covers. "This is it, Lottie. Give it all you've got."

A long moan and an extra-long minute of pushing, and the sound of a newborn filled the room. The atmosphere in the room changed immediately from anxiety to joy as a new baby boy joined the family.

Zach went to the bedside and placed his head on the pillow next to his wife. "You did it again, Lottie-girl. He's a fine young Amish lad, that's for sure."

Cindy had Zach tie the umbilical cord and then continued to handle the next stage of the delivery. Anna stood by and watched the events transpire and then went over to Lottie and Zach and kissed them. "He's a beautiful boppli. Congratulations to you both."

A new birth was always a thrill. And perhaps with God's blessing, she would one day deliver a child for Abe.

When she got back to the house, Abe was pacing the floor. "Anna, I feared something was wrong. You were gone over an hour."

After she told him about the new baby, he grinned and nodded. "No wonder you were late. What a nice surprise for you."

"I'm especially glad it's over, because Lottie was having a difficult pregnancy. Everything went so gut. He's adorable." She went and put her hands in his. "Maybe it will be me someday."

"Jah, Anna. That would be wonderful-gut."

"Not yet, though."

"Nee, not yet. So I lost real quick at Monopoly. They're still playing."

"I'd better go next door and help with the kinner until Lottie's mamm gets there. The mid-wife lives only a few houses away from her parents and she can tell them about the birth."

"With everything that's going on, maybe I can sleep on your sofa tonight. You think it would be okay?"

"I guess so. It would probably be all right. After all, we're adults and we know we're not doing anything wrong."

"You're right. I just don't want your character questioned. In the meantime, you go back and help your family. I'll make the kids sandwiches, Anna. We'll be just fine."

With this, Luke came into the kitchen. "I can't believe it! Rachel beat us and she's still sick. A maed! How embarrassing is that?"

Anna laughed. "Very. Abe's going to stay here with you. I have to go next door. You have a new cousin. Tell him, Abe. I need to get back there."

As she left, she heard Abe suggest they play another game. What a good thing he was there to help out. God always saw to it. His timing was perfect. Though she didn't understand some of life's problems, this she knew in her heart. God was in charge and he watched over her each and every day. The questions she did have would have to wait. That was for sure.

Chapter Twenty

After the strain of Rachel's illness and hospital stay, Anna felt totally drained. The first evening at home, even though Abe was there with her, she kept nodding and slipping into sleep as she sat on the couch with him after the children were all in bed.

"Anna," she heard Abe say softly. "You need to get your sleep. Go on upstairs and I'll make myself comfortable on your sofa and catch a few winks myself."

She forced her eyes open and covered a yawn. "I'm sorry. I hoped we'd have time to talk now that the kinner are down."

"Tomorrow, we'll have more time. All I need is a blanket or quilt and I'll be all set."

"There's the quilt we brought Rachel home in. I folded it and put it on the rocker in the corner. There's a small pillow you can use next to it."

"Yah. Right in front of my eyes." He stood and reached for her hands. She rose and he placed his arms around her. "I'm glad you have your little angel back home with you. Now you go have happy dreams."

"Denki. I think I'll sleep pretty gut tonight. I haven't heard Rachel cough at all since she went to bed."

"If I hear her, I can go up and see what she wants."

"Nee, that's okay. My room is right next to hers. I'll hear her. You get some gut sleep yourself, Abe."

Anna slept through until seven in the morning. Even the boys managed to be quiet until their first quarrel over orange juice woke everyone up.

Abe joined Luke when he went out to milk Barbie, the cow. Luke insisted on doing everything himself and Abe merely stood back and watched.

"She ain't giving much anymore," Luke mentioned as he struggled to get the last drops.

"She looks old."

"She is, but she's a gut old cow. Onkel Zach gives us extra milk when we need it."

"Nice to have him next door," Abe said, fearing the boy's reaction to leaving once his mother re-married. That wasn't going to make things any easier.

"Jah. Do you love my mamm?" he asked unexpectedly.

"I think I do, Sohn. It may take a while for her to love me back."

"I don't think she ever will. She was real close to my daed and she still cries sometimes."

Abe nodded. "I understand. Luke, if we marry—and I believe we will—I'm not going to try to take your dat's place in your life, but I would want to be a gut father figure for you and your bruders and schwester."

Luke's brows rose and he stiffened. "We get along okay the way it is. We don't need a father figure."

"Maybe you don't think you do, but your bruders are younger. And look at Rachel. She's just a young maed."

"You'd probably have boppli, wouldn't you?" he asked, staring into Abe's eyes, almost as a challenge.

"It might happen. Jah." Abe's jaw was strained.

"That's what I thought."

"There's nothing wrong with a husband and wife wanting kinner, you know."

Luke's eyes filled as he nodded half-heartedly.

"Look, your mamm is a young woman. Should she go the rest of her life alone? Don't you want her to find happiness someday?"

"She's happy already. She has us."

"You're too young to understand, Luke. Someday you will, but—"

"I know about that stuff. I'm not stupid you know. Guys talk."

"Well, Gott wouldn't have made Adam and Eve the way he did if he didn't want them to multiply the way they did. It's not wrong or dirty."

"I guess. I still think my mudder would hate to… you know."

"I think this is a discussion you may want to leave alone now, Luke. As adults, your mudder and me are gonna make the decisions about the future. We want you all to be happy about it, but we have to do what's best for everyone."

"I'm done now." Luke lifted the partially filled metal container with the milk and lugged it towards the barn door.

"Want any help?" Abe asked, following.

"Nee. I don't need anyone's help."

As Abe followed the young boy into the house, he

wondered if he'd handled it well. Somehow he had to reach this hurting young man. So far, it didn't look as if he'd made any progress.

Anna had Luke pour the milk into glass bottles and store them in the refrigerator. Abe sat at the table. She looked from Luke's scowling expression to Abe's serious face. Oh dear, things didn't look too good. "I'm frying *panhaas*. Luke, do you want any?"

"Nee. I'm not hungry."

"Abe?"

"Jah, that would be nice. Just two pieces, bitte."

Rachel came into the room, fully dressed. She walked over to Abe. "Look, my giraffe is smiling. He's happy cuz I'm all better."

Abe smiled and patted Rachel's head. "He sure does look happy."

Anna looked over as she waited for the iron pan to heat up more. "You may feel gut, Rachel, but you need to rest for a few more days. The doctor told us, remember?"

"Jah, but my cough is way better now."

"It's amazing, ain't it?" Anna asked Abe as she took a seat at the table.

"Gut doctor."

"Jah, and a gut Gott."

"You can say that again," Abe said, nodding his head in agreement.

Luke left the room as his two younger brothers came tearing into the kitchen.

"Buwe, what have I told you about running in the house?" Anna said as she drew her brows together.

"You love it, right Mamm?" Mark said, mischievously.

Anna rolled her eyes and looked over at Abe, who looked uncertain about what to say. So he said nothing.

"I want panhaas, too," Matthew said as he watched his mother place slices of the pork scrapple into the pan.

"I know. I'm making extra for you and Mark."

"Luke will want some," Matthew said as he walked over to the stove to watch his mother as she pushed the pieces of ground-up pork scraps and trimmings mixed with buckwheat flour.

"My bruder made the panhaas. He puts lot of spice into it. Hope you'll like it," Anna said looking over at Abe.

"Just the way we make it back home."

"When are you going home?" Mark asked Abe as he took a seat across the table from him.

"That's not polite, Mark," Anna said quickly.

"That's okay. He has a right to ask," Abe said. "As soon as things are normal here."

"They're normal now," Mark said.

Anna let out a long sigh. "There's no rush for Abe to leave, Mark. He's been kind enough to come to help us out."

Luke walked into the room. He went over to the pan and peered in. "Did you make enough for me? I'm hungry now."

"I can fry more."

"Give him my pieces, Anna," Abe said. "I can wait."

"Nee, I don't want yours!"

Anna's mouth dropped open as she stared at her son. "Go to your room, Luke. Now."

"I don't have to." He folded his arms and glared at this mother.

"Luke, your mudder wants you to go to your room. Go now."

"You can't tell me what to do!" he said, his eyes filling up as he raised his voice.

Anna put her hands over her eyes and shook her head. "Oh, Abe, I'm sorry."

He rose and walked over to Luke, who took a step back to avoid being touched.

"Luke," Abe said quietly, "This is not the way to show respect for your mother. See how upset you've made her. Please leave the room and the three of us will discuss your behavior later."

Luke's body was rigid as he looked from Abe to his mother. "You're gonna marry him, aren't you? He's gonna boss us all around, isn't he? And you don't care! What would Daed say?"

Mark and Matthew sat silently looking on.

Rachel's head was leaning on her arms. She raised it and looked over at Luke. "You're being a dummkopf. Abe and Mamm need each other. They're real, real lonely and you're selfish and mean. Besides, I want a dat again."

Anna went and laid her hands on Rachel's shoulders. "Your bruder isn't stupid, honey, but he is acting very rude."

Luke looked around at the family as they sat stunned, waiting for his next move. Slowly, he turned and left the room. They could hear him as he climbed the stairs to his room.

"Wow!" Mark said. "I guess you won't want us for kids now," he added as he looked over at Abe, who had walked over to the stove and stood with his arms folded.

"It's not easy on anyone," he answered quietly. "But we need to pray about it and ask the gut Lord to help us do the right thing."

"I don't mind if you marry Mamm," Matthew said. "I think she smiles more when you're here."

"Not today," Mark said. "Look at her. She's a mess."

In spite of her feelings at the moment, Anna laughed out loud. The boys joined her. Abe didn't laugh, but he smiled over at Matthew. "Your Mamm has been through a lot of heartache. It would be best if you buwe remember that and do what you can to help her."

"I get the eggs," Matthew said.

"And we both get firewood," Mark added.

"And that's very gut, but you must do more." Abe took his seat again as Anna turned the browning patties. "You have to listen to your mudder and do as she tells you, even when you don't want to."

"Would you beat us if you marry Mamm?" Mark asked.

"Nee, I don't beat children, but I would punish you if you disobeyed."

"How?" Matthew asked.

"Buwe, leave Abe alone," Anna said, shaking her head.

"It's okay, Anna. They have a right to ask. Let's put it this way. If we marry, there will be seven kinner living in one house. If we are to have order, and not chaos, I would have to take charge with your mudder as my partner. We would have to be strict in order to survive."

"Sounds like spanking to me," Matthew said.

"If all else fails…"

"I like Benny," Mark said, tilting his head, "but John ain't nice to us."

"He'll be treated the same way you are. If he misbehaves, he'll pay the consequences," Abe continued.

"You'd treat him better," Matthew said as he reached for his glass of juice.

"We'd treat you all the same," Anna said, breaking into the discussion.

"Could I go live with Aenti Lottie if I don't like it here anymore?" Mark asked.

"Nee. We will all remain together." Anna turned the flame down as she removed the meat from the pan and laid it on paper towels to drain off the fat.

"What about Allie?" Rachel asked.

"She'll be part of the family, too," Abe said.

"She may not like it here in Pennsylvania," Rachel added.

Abe looked over at Anna. How much should they tell the children?

Anna shook her head towards him, almost imperceptibly to the others, but Abe understood and made no further comment. After breakfast, without Luke there, he suggested the younger boys go outside with him while he groomed the horse.

Rachel was disappointed that she had to remain inside, but she sat and worked on a potholder she was making on a small metal frame. The colorful fabrics kept her occupied as she wove them together.

Anna poured herself another cup of coffee and sat alone. So many issues. How could they possibly meld two such different families together? Maybe it wouldn't work. A tear ran down her cheek and she pressed her sleeve against her face. And then she prayed silently for guidance.

Chapter Twenty-One

Around noon, Beth and Anna's parents arrived for the main meal. Abe greeted them warmly, though Beth seemed distant as she responded.

"We just went to see our new boppli next door. My, he's a cutie," Rose said as she hung up her jacket. "He weighs over nine pounds."

"Jah, he looked big," Anna said, smiling over at her mother. "Sit everyone. I have meatloaf in the oven. It will be a half hour before it's ready."

"Where are the buwe?" her father asked as he placed his hat over a peg by the door.

"Outside playing with their cousins."

"Guess they're in the back. Nice to have quiet," he added.

"Oh, jah," Anna said, glancing over at Abe, who remained non-committal. They'd had very little time to themselves since the morning started.

"I have to go see Rachel," her mother said. "Is she in her room?"

"Jah, she wanted to play school with her dolls."

"So Abe," Beth said, turning towards him, "When are you going back to Ohio?"

"Uh, I'm going to try to get the driver for tomorrow."

Anna looked over in surprise. They hadn't discussed his departure. Had he made it sooner than he'd wanted after the display of disobedience from her boys? Her heart pounded as she feared the worst. Her mother returned to the kitchen and sat across from Anna, next to Beth. Isaiah took the end seat.

"I guess your kinner must miss you," Beth added.

"They're being watched by my schwester and her husband. I'm sure they're just fine."

Anna checked the mashed potatoes and set them back on a hot spot to stay warm. Corn was heating on the front burner. She took a seat next to Abe.

There was silence for several moments. Then Anna cleared her throat. "Abe and I have decided to marry, right?" She looked over, dreading his response.

He nodded and smiled at her. "Jah, you're right about that." He looked over at her parents. "You have a wonderful-gut dochder, as you know. I will try to make her happy."

Isaiah nodded and pulled his beard. "You're taking on a whole family."

"Jah, we both are," he said.

"Well, we'll be here to help out," Rose said, smiling over.

Anna and Abe exchanged glances. *Here we go*, Anna thought to herself.

"Mamm, we... I...we've decided to settle in Ohio."

Rose's hand went to her mouth as she shuddered. Isaiah merely looked straight ahead.

Beth pulled on her kapp strings. "Is this what *you* want, Anna?"

"We think it's the wisest move."

Rose found her tongue. "Usually a man will move to the maed's district, where she's been baptized."

"Mamm, we've discussed it, Abe and me. His farm is larger and he's got all his livestock. Besides, his youngest, Allie, needs a familiar setting. It's going to be difficult enough for the child to accept me and my kinner, without being in a new house. She's so used to Abe's schwester taking care of her..."

"I think it's wrong," Beth finally managed to say.

"Beth, it's not your decision," Anna said, glaring at her sister. "We've discussed it and it feels like the right way to handle things."

"Have you told your kinner?" Beth continued, avoiding Abe.

"Not yet, but we will. We have time."

"How much time?" Rose asked, her mouth twisted.

"We haven't set a date yet," Anna answered.

Abe coughed into his hand and then said, "Soon. We hope real soon. There's no point in waiting."

"The point would be," Beth started, as she turned her eyes to his, "to get to know each other better and help the kinner adjust to the whole idea. They've all been through so much."

"That's the reason for not waiting too long," he said. "They'll get too used to things the way they are, and it would be better for all concerned to have a mudder and a daed together raising them."

"I agree with that," Isaiah said, thoughtfully. "Beth,

you leave it to Anna and Abe. They know what they're doing."

"But—"

"No buts. Stay out of it."

Beth stood abruptly and went over to the stove where she stirred the corn.

"Beth, this ain't an easy decision for us," Anna started. "We just want to do the best thing for everyone concerned."

"Not for me or your parents," Beth said, angrily. "I have to put my kinner first."

"And yourself, obviously."

"That's unfair!"

"It's true. You probably just can't stand being without a man!"

Isaiah glared at his younger daughter. "Beth, you've said way too much. Mind your mouth."

Rose scowled at Beth as well. "You certainly have a way about you, Beth. You always manage to say the wrong thing."

"Right! That's why I'm single and glad of it!" She put the spoon down, grabbed her shawl, and left the house.

"Sorry, Abe. That's my schwester."

"It's okay. She loves you and your kinner. I understand." He looked over at Isaiah and Rose. "It was not an easy decision. It could have gone either way. I was willing to move, but when we sorted out all the problems, and looked at the gut as well as the bad, it made more sense to settle in Ohio."

Isaiah sat back and moved his hands to his suspenders, tucking his thumbs behind them. "We'll sure miss you, Anna. And the kinner."

"It's not that long a trip, Daed," she said, her voice wavering. "I'd sure expect you and Mamm to visit."

Rose blew her nose and tucked her hankie in her apron pocket. She made every effort to smile. "Sure, and you can come visit us, too. Like on holidays?"

"Jah, but it would be better if you come to Ohio," Anna said. "Easier, you know."

"I'd be happy to pay the driver," Abe added.

Isaiah grimaced. "Nee, I have the money."

"I didn't mean—"

"I know. I know," Isaiah said. "Sorry, this is just all a bit of a shock."

"I understand," Abe said.

"Do you love our dochder?" Rose asked, sniffling.

"I believe I do. It's early yet, but she's a mighty fine woman and I respect her very much."

"She ain't had it easy," Isaiah said. "Neither have the kinner."

"Nor have mine," Abe added.

"You're taking on a big responsibility," Isaiah continued. "You've thought it through?"

"Jah, we have both thought it through, right, Anna?"

She shook her head. Somehow she was able to keep her tears from flowing, though it had been even more difficult than she had anticipated. And the children had to be told yet.

"Then if it be Gott's will, we will accept it, won't we, Rose?" Isaiah looked over at his wife.

She nodded. "I'll get used to the idea, I guess. When you have boppli, I'll come pay you a visit."

Anna's face flushed. "That won't be for awhile, I'm sure and certain of that."

Her father's brows rose. He looked from Anna to

Abe. Then he looked down at the table in front of him. "Guess that meatloaf should be done soon, Anna."

"I'll check it, Daed."

"I'll go look for Beth," Rose said, rising.

"She's by the barn. I can see her from here," Isaiah said, looking out the kitchen window. "Let her cool off a little longer. Ever since she and Josiah broke up, she's been testy."

"We've been so close, Daed," Anna started. "It's not going to be easy on either of us to be separated. I hope if she doesn't get a job, that she'll pay us a long visit."

"She won't until you have your families all settled down," Rose said. "You know she has little patience for disobedient kinner."

"Jah, how well I know."

Beth paced back and forth in front of the barn. How could he take Anna away from her family? What kind of man would think so little of the woman he was to marry as to ask her to forsake all her family and friends? Why on earth would Anna agree to it, anyway? Was she so desperate to have a man in her life that everything else paled in comparison? Beth was glad she wasn't like that. No way. No man would be that important to her to have her turn her back on her loved ones.

Abe seemed like a decent man, though. He was nice to the kinner. At least at this stage. He could be just trying to make a good impression. And then when the vows are said…

Could it be that Beth was jealous? Was part of this anger really towards her own state of affairs? She had so hoped Josiah was the right man for her. After she got her eyes opened about Randy and saw what a no-good human being he was, she had seen Josiah in a new light. She appreciated his intellect, his honesty, his thoughtful ways. And when they kissed, she had felt a new feeling. A desire for more intimacy. Strange, but she wished now, she'd never felt anything for the man. It would be far easier to accept her life the way it was if she'd never had expectations of something more.

The ads in the paper never seemed right for her skills. She really didn't want to be a nanny to some bratty kids. Teaching had taught her that. Patience was a virtue she was not endowed with, unfortunately. Too bad it hadn't worked out with Josiah. It would have been better to have remained friends. She'd still have her job, it she hadn't allowed her emotions to take hold.

If Anna did marry Abe and move away, maybe she would pay them a long visit and just get away from everything here. It might be good for her and she could help with the children. Ugh. Not a good idea. Here a man had come into her sister's life and offered to care for and help raise Anna's children. Beth should be delighted for her sister—not putting a wedge in their relationship. What kind of a sister was she anyway?

As she turned for the fifth time by the corner of the barn, she berated herself. There was still time to make amends with Abe. Surely, she could find the right words to set things right with the man who would become her brother-in-law. It was important for her relationship with Anna, to accept Abe. She'd apologize and give her support for their decision.

Satisfied with her plans, Beth walked towards the house just as a buggy turned on the drive. Oh my goodness! It was Josiah Yoder. Now what could he want?

* * *

Beth stood waiting as Josiah stopped and tethered his horse. He nodded in her direction and then walked over and gave her a forced smile.

"Hi," she said, folding her arms. "Problems?"

"Nee, I stopped by to see how Rachel was doing. Is she still in the hospital?"

"She came home yesterday."

"Oh, that's wonderful. I'm so glad."

"Jah, me too. You want to say hullo to her?"

"Sure."

She turned towards the house and he stepped quickly to reach her side. "So how have you been, Beth? You must be relieved."

"Of course, I'm relieved. Except now I've learned that my dear schwester is moving to Ohio."

"Really?"

"Jah, she's going to marry that fellow I told you about."

"Well, I'll be. They hardly know each other."

"He came to be near her when he heard about Rachel."

"That was nice. He must care a lot."

"Josiah, if he didn't care a lot, he wouldn't be marrying her now, would he?"

He let out a short laugh. "You've made your point, Beth. So have you found a job yet?"

"Nee, but with Rachel sick and all, I haven't had time really."

"I guess not."

They stopped and turned towards each other before climbing the steps to the kitchen from the porch. He took his hat off and gripped it with both hands. "I don't suppose you'd consider working for me again, would you?"

"Are you serious?"

"Jah, it ain't a joke. You're a gut worker. If we kept things simple—just employer and employee—nothing more?"

"I don't know. Let me think about it."

"Take your time, though I may have to put an ad in this week since it's getting busier all the time. I have to stay up till late sometimes to get the shop work done."

"Congratulations. I guess that must please you."

"It does, in a way."

"I'd want a raise," she said, surprising herself at her audacity.

"Sure. You'd deserve it," he said, nodding. They climbed the steps and Beth pushed the door open.

"Set another place. Josiah's here."

Rose's mouth dropped open. One surprise after another. How much can one person take? Anna nodded towards Josiah as Beth introduced him to Abe. The men shook hands and began speaking man-talk while Beth went over to the stove where Anna was slicing the meatloaf. "I'm sorry I acted the way I did. Forgive me?"

Anna turned and gave her sister a hug. "Of course. I understand. Believe me, Beth, I'll miss you tons and tons."

"Well don't get me started. I sure don't need to cry in front of everyone."

"Did you know Josiah was going to come by?"

"No idea. He came to find out about Rachel."

"That was real nice of him."

"Jah, and he wants me to come back to work for him."

"Seriously? Wow. What did you tell him?"

"That I'd think about it."

"And did you?"

"Jah. All of one minute."

"And?"

Beth leaned over and whispered in her sister's ear. "He's giving me a raise. Jah, I'm gonna get my job back, but that's all it is. A job."

"Oh, jah, that's for sure."

"And for certain." Beth winked at her sister and strained the corn into a serving bowl.

Chapter Twenty-Two

Josiah only stayed a few minutes after the meal was finished, explaining he was behind on his commitments. Before he left, Beth told him she'd take him up on the job offer. He grinned and asked when she could start.

"How about Monday?"

"Gut. Denki. I really appreciate it." Then he offered to have Abe stop at the shop to use his phone so he could set up his ride home.

"I'll drive him over later," Anna said.

Isaiah and Rose asked Abe to sit and talk about his farm, leaving Beth and Anna alone in the kitchen.

"I know Abe is concerned about you, Beth."

"Why should he be? I'm a big girl. I can handle whatever comes my way."

"Well, he knows how close we are."

"Anna, Abe is a nice guy. I'm glad you met him. I'm really sorry for my behavior. I want to apologize to him for the way I acted."

"It's really okay. He doesn't expect you to apologize. He understands how you feel. By the way, I have to admit, I'm pleased that you're going to be working for Josiah again. Maybe things will—"

"I know you don't believe me, but I don't care about that. I just need a job and I liked working in the showroom. It was fun and I think I did a gut job."

"I'm sure you did. He wouldn't ask you to come back if you weren't a gut employee."

"Oh. I guess you're right."

Anna looked over at her sister. Why did she sound disappointed. "Not that that's the only reason he wants you back, but maybe—"

"Nee, you're absolutely right. He needed someone to fill the job and I was already trained. Of course, it makes sense."

"Beth, are you disappointed? Maybe a tad?"

"Not even a tad."

"Beth, you shouldn't lie. Especially to me."

"Okay, maybe just a tad. But that's all. I guess I won't be visiting you for a while, Anna, now that I'll be working again. Do you think you'll be able to come see us sometimes, even without all the kinner?"

"I can't answer that. We're not even married yet. I don't know how things are going to work out."

"You'll be busy, that's for sure."

"Oh, jah."

"If you have more kinner—"

"Hopefully not for a while."

"You've discussed it?"

"Not in detail. Someday we'll probably have a boppli, but I'm not ready yet for that, and neither is Abe."

"Good to get those things straightened out ahead of time."

"I guess so. It's awkward though. We haven't known each other that long. He told me he's falling in love with me though."

"Anna, that's great! And you? How do you feel about him?"

"I can't say for sure. I care about him—a lot. He's so gut to me and the kinner. So far, anyway."

"Maybe love will follow. I hope so."

"In time."

Rachel came into the kitchen as they finished redding it up and she pulled on her mother's skirt. "I'm tired, Mamm. Can I go to bed?"

"Oh honey, of course. I should have taken you up sooner."

"I wasn't tired before."

"Do you want me to put her to bed for you, Anna?"

"Nee, please, Mamm, I want you to put me to bed," Rachel begged.

"Very well. I'd better do it. She's been clingy ever since she got sick."

"It's okay. Glad you're feeling better, Rachel."

"Denki. Don't be upset, Aenti. I love you, too."

Beth grinned. "Liebschdi, you know I love you. Sweet dreams."

When Beth went home with her parents, she told her mother about her decision to work for Josiah again. Rose grinned. "Wise move, Beth. He's a fine young man."

"It doesn't mean we're going to go out together, Mamm. Don't make too much out of it."

"I'm just glad you two aren't holding grudges. That's not the Amish way."

"Nee, no grudges, but I'm not going to give my heart away this time, and if I have a chance to date a nice Amish man in the future, I'll probably take him up on it. I'd like to have at least two children someday."

"Two? Mercy, you'd be an odd Amish woman with only two kinner."

Beth rolled her eyes. "I've been an odd Amish woman all my life. Why stop now?" she asked her mother, who grinned and nodded over at her smiling daughter.

All the way home to Ohio, Abe thought about Anna and the children. They were a handful. It wasn't going to be easy, but in the end it would benefit everyone—he hoped. If it weren't for his own children, he'd not even consider marrying again. Or would he? He pictured Anna's sweet smile and heard her soft voice. What a lovely woman she was. He really was falling in love. It wouldn't be the same as it was with Mary. It couldn't be. They'd known each other their whole lives. There'd never been anyone else in his life. And now Anna. Strange. He hadn't thought it possible to love another woman—ever. Was it desire? Was he merely using the children as an excuse because he wanted to be with a woman again? Mercy, he hoped not. Besides, they would not become intimate for a while. Probably a long while. He'd leave that up to Anna.

This week he'd go to the bishop and the district deacon to make arrangements for the wedding. It would be small—just immediate family. No huge reception. Not for this second marriage. He had discussed it briefly with Anna and she was in agreement. Her bishop would be notified and any paper work could be taken care of immediately so they wouldn't have to delay the wedding. Hopefully, he'd send off the *Zeugnis* to acknowledge that Anna was a member in good standing with her church. Though most Amish weddings took place in fall and early winter, he felt sure his bishop would take his situation into account and marry them when the details were sorted out. They'd been friends for years—even before Timothy Zook became his bishop. The men were only two years apart in age. Tim was there for him every step of the way after the accident. God had selected the right man when he chose Tim to become their bishop.

The trip seemed longer than usual. His driver Tom had come out to get him right away, but he obviously had driven part of the night and was weary from travel. They talked a little, but then Tom concentrated on his driving while Abe used the quiet time to meditate and pray. He asked for guidance, as he always did, and blessings for Anna and her children as well as his own. He hoped the fears that occasionally popped into his head were unjustified. He wanted this arrangement to work out and wanted it with all his heart.

The boys ran over to him as soon as he arrived at Naomi's. He grabbed them and swung them around. Allie sat on the sofa watching, her little eyes full of wonder. He set the boys down, knelt, and extended his arms to her. She moved slowly off the couch and allowed her father to embrace her. Naomi stood watching and nodded to her brother. "She's been fussy since you left. I think she missed you."

Abe looked over as he released her. "Hard to believe. She doesn't make much of a fuss over me when I'm here."

"But she looks for your hugs, Abe. I can tell. How was your trip?" she asked as he took off his jacket and set it on a peg by the door.

"Gut. Real gut. Rachel came home from the hospital a couple days ago and she's much better. Hardly coughs anymore. It was scary for a while though—especially for Anna. I'm glad I made the trip."

"Oh jah, I'm sure it helped to have your support. She told me how hard it's been doing things on her own."

"I guess I may as well tell you now. We're going to marry."

Naomi grinned widely. "Jah? That's wonderful-gut. I think she's a real special person and will make a gut mudder for your little ones."

"I agree."

"And her kinner? They're gut for you?"

Abe chuckled. "When they want to be, but it's hard right now. I don't have any authority over them and they know it. The oldest bu, Luke, is the only one I think we'll have a problem with."

"And your John. He ain't real happy thinking you might re-marry. Best you tell him soon though."

"One piece of news that may help. Anna and I will live here."

"Oh, I'm so glad. It wonders me why she was willing to move."

"The main reason was her concern for Allie. She felt it would be too much for the maed to have to adapt to new surroundings as well as a new mamm."

"That speaks well of Anna. She's very thoughtful of others."

Abe nodded. "Jah, she's a fine woman."

"Do you think you could love her in time?"

"Jah, I do. I already care a lot about her. In fact, I believe I'm falling in love with her. I even told her that."

"My goodness. What did she say?"

"Not too much. She seemed pleased, but she didn't say how she felt."

"Maybe it's expecting too much too soon."

"Probably. In the gut Lord's time."

"Jah, bruder. That's the way it has to be."

Monday morning Beth got to Josiah's at eight o'clock. The front door was locked so she went around the back to his private entrance. When she knocked, he opened the door and looked surprised.

"Did you forget I was working today?" she asked as she removed her boots and came through the door.

"Nee, but you used to come in later. Just surprised is all."

"I figured we'd need time to go over the books and paperwork since it's probably piled up since I was here."

He grinned. "You're right about that. Whew, I'm so behind, Beth, you won't believe it."

"Oh, I believe it all right."

"Want some kaffi?"

"Sure. Hope you've washed the pot out since I was here."

He laughed as he turned towards the burner to get the coffeepot. "I think once I accidentally ran it under the faucet. I stopped Saturday at one of the bakeries in town to pick up some sticky buns. There's one left. Do you want it?"

"I'll split it with you. Is it stale yet?"

"Hope not." He reached in a paper toot and took out the bun and laid it on a plate before cutting it. "There. You choose."

"I'll take the smaller piece. I'm not particularly hungry. Mamm made pancakes this morning."

"So how is Rachel doing?" he asked.

"Last I heard, she's just about normal."

"Abe seems like a nice man. Think they'll marry soon?"

"They plan to. She's moving to Ohio."

Abe placed the dishes at the small table and motioned for Beth to sit. When the coffee was ready, he set the pot on a tile in the middle of the table and sat across from her.

"I bet that's gonna be tough on you."

Beth looked down at her plate and nodded. "As long as they're happy. That what counts."

"Jah, you're right. Maybe I can get back there and introduce them to some people I know."

"I don't think that will be necessary. Her best friend moved there a while back and she knows Abe's family already. Plus, she'll be so busy raising all those kinner, she won't have time to get lonely."

"But you will," he said, glancing at her expression.

"Mmm. This bun is still gut. Denki."

"So, Beth, have you made any new friends yourself?"

"If you mean male friends, nee."

"Actually… I wasn't thinking…"

"Sure you were. Well, when we're done here, I'll get things organized again. Any new projects?"

"A couple. I'm interviewing a couple guys this week

to look for another carpenter to help me out. It's too much for one man."

"Already? I'm amazed at how quickly your business is growing."

"So am I. Gott is gut."

"Jah, He is." She stood as she popped the end of the bun into her mouth and took her dirty plate and mug to the sink. There was a small pile of soiled dishes already resting there.

"Leave them, Beth. I'll get them later."

"I will leave them. I need to get busy with the important stuff before I bail you out here."

He laughed. "Good ole Beth. You never change."

"I guess I should," she said with a sigh.

"Don't you dare," Josiah said as he followed her into the front. "I'd have to fire you and look for someone else."

Chapter Twenty-Three

Anna knew she had to divulge her plans to her children about the move to Ohio after she married Abe. She prayed intensely for God to prepare their hearts and minds for the life-changing days ahead. She also prayed for guidance with the right words when she told them of her plans. Finally, one rainy day when the boys seemed in a cooperative mood, she decided it was time.

It was chilly in the house and the children were gathered around the coal stove in the kitchen putting a large puzzle together on the floor.

"I'm going to make donuts later, but first I'd like you all to come in the sitting room with me," Anna said, wiping her hands on her dishcloth as she set it aside.

"I wanna help make donuts," Rachel said as she reached for Anna's hand. They walked out of the room.

"You will help," Anna said.

After a few complaints verbalized, the boys followed and plunked themselves down on the floor. Anna and Rachel sat on the sofa.

"It's about Abe, ain't it?" Luke asked with a frown on his face.

"Partly. You all know we're planning on marrying in March or early April."

Everyone nodded, their eyes wide with curiosity. What would be next?

Anna cleared her throat. "Well, we decided to set up house at Abe's."

"No way," Luke sputtered. "That ain't fair! Why's he making us move?"

"It was actually my suggestion."

Silence followed her statement as the children processed this unwanted news. Finally, Mark wiped his eyes with his shirt sleeve. "I'm gonna miss my cousins."

"And grossmammi," Rachel added, a tear running down her cheek.

"And grossdawdi," Matthew added, choking back his own tears.

"We'll still see them," Anna said as she tried to find the words to console them.

"It ain't the same, Mamm, and you know it," Luke said.

"We'll have a new family, you guys," Mark said. "And new bruders."

"And a new schwester," Rachel said, her tears all but ceasing. Anna wiped them away from her face with a tissue and put her arm around her. "Yah, we have to look at the gut things."

"And Abe will love us like his own kinner, right, Mamm?" Rachel's eyes implored Anna to confirm this most important fact.

"Oh, jah. Abe is a gut man and he will do everything he can to make this work."

"And if it doesn't?" Luke asked, twisting a lock of his blonde hair around a finger.

"It has to work, Sohn," Anna said, looking over.

"I'll just run away," Luke said as he dropped his hand and defiantly folded his arms. He stared at his mother.

"Luke, why would you say such a thing? You know how hard it's been since your daed passed away. Don't you want to have a dat?"

Luke turned from her gaze and looked down at the floor. "I had the best one, and Gott took him away. I don't need Abe."

"I think you do. We all need Abe," Anna said softly.

"I'll take care of Abe's dochter, Mamm," Rachel said. "She's gonna need a big schwester."

"That's right. She will. Think of the fun we'll have. We can have picnics in the spring and go to church together—"

"We can do that here. We don't have to go all the way to Ohio," Luke said. "Can't you change your mind? I won't have any friends."

"Of course you will. You're a very friendly bu and people will like you and want you as their friend."

"Oh right," he said, glaring at the floor again.

"We'll all have friends," Mark said. "Benny and John will see to that."

"Don't be a dumpkoff," Luke said angrily. "John is weird. He has his own friends and he doesn't need us."

"Well, Benny's nice," Matthew added.

"Sure, you guys will be fine. But not me."

"Luke, you have to make an effort," Anna began. "I

think you and John could end up being best of friends, but it will mean some cooperation on your part."

"And his," he said, biting his lower lip.

"Can we come back a lot to visit, Mamm?" Rachel asked.

"I hope it works out to do just that. And the family can come visit us whenever it's possible."

"Aenti Beth is gonna be mad at you," Rachel said.

"She wants us to be happy," Anna said with a nod.

"What makes you think you'll be happy?" Luke asked. "Maybe Abe just needs a housekeeper."

Anna shook her head. "I'm sure it will help to have a fraa, but it's more than a housecleaner he needs."

"And a mudder for his kinner," he continued.

"That may be part of it," Anna admitted.

"And sex."

"Luke! Shame on you. You can go to your room now and stay there until you repent."

Mark and Matthew put their heads together and giggled, but Rachel looked up at her mother, questioning.

"Your bruder is very naughty, Rachel. Don't let that sit in your head."

"It's silly," Rachel said, turning towards Luke. "You say really crazy words."

"Luke…I asked you to go to your room."

He rose slowly and without turning, went up the stairs to his room. Anna looked at her other boys. "I want you to scrub that from your heads. Luke is not behaving gut at all."

"Abe just needs a mudder for his kinner, right?" Mark asked quietly. "Not that other stuff."

"Abe needs a woman to take care of his family. Yah, Mark. We won't discuss other stuff, if you don't mind.

Now, Rachel and I have a project. Those donuts don't make themselves. You can go back to your puzzle if you'd like."

They returned to the kitchen. It had been challenging. Luke might present real problems, but she was glad they knew about the move. She wondered if Abe had told his family yet. The one thing that was difficult for her was not having a way to communicate with Abe. Perhaps his bishop would be more liberal and allow cell phones. Tomorrow she planned to go to Josiah's workshop to wait for Abe's call. They arranged to talk every Wednesday around noon. She counted the hours.

Abe made his way to Bishop Tim's farmhouse to talk about the wedding. He laid the reins aside upon seeing Tim's wife, Hazel, hanging diapers on the lines. Though it still went down below freezing many nights, the days were beginning to warm and the Amish women preferred the fresh smells of the outdoors to their cellars. With six young children, Hazel washed more frequently than some of the older women. It appeared she was expecting again. She smiled and waved as he tethered the horse to the post. After going over and greeting her, he turned towards the horse stable. Tim stood outside with a grooming brush in his hands. He laid it down and brushed his hand off on his workpants before shaking Abe's hand.

"Didn't expect to see you today, Abe. What's up?"

"A lot actually."

"Come on in. Time for kaffi and Hazel's mudder stopped by earlier with a batch of fresh butterscotch chip cookies."

Abe walked alongside his friend and grinned. "One of my favorites." Then his smile turned down. "Mary made the best."

"Oh jah, I remember hers were almost as gut as Hazel's," he said, attempting to raise Abe's spirits.

After pouring them each a mug of coffee, they sat at the long trestle table to talk. The little ones ran in and out of the room creating a bit of a racket. "Sorry. The kinner are getting mighty restless. Thinking this weather better improve soon. Poor Hazel is wore out."

"She in a family way?"

"Oh jah. Well we have a couple months left. After six maedel I'm kinda hoping for a bu."

Abe nodded. "It would be nice."

"How's that little one doing? Alice?"

"Not so gut. I mean she's healthy and all, but she still won't live with me and the buwe."

"That could be a problem."

"It's a major problem. Mary would not be takin' to it real kindly if she knew."

"Gut thing you have Naomi." Tim passed the plate of cookies over to Abe. "Take a couple. One ain't gonna do it."

Abe obliged and set them next to his mug.

"I had an amazing thing happen a couple months ago."

Tim looked up, brows raised. "Oh jah? Wanna talk about it?"

Abe preceded to tell him about meeting Anna. He explained how she had been praying for him and his family ever since the accident. Tim kept nodding, but kept quiet as Abe told his story. "So we really like each other a whole lot and we want to marry. Soon."

"And you want a mudder for your kinner."

"Jah."

"And she wants a daed for hers."

"Jah."

Tim pulled on his red beard and pushed back in his chair. "Think that's enough?"

"Tim, it's all I can promise. I may be getting strong feelings for Anna and I think she likes me well enough. It just seems like the right time in my life to do it."

"And the buwe?"

"I haven't told them yet. I don't need their permission to marry, you know."

"I realize that, but there may be problems melding the two families together."

"We know that. Anna and I have talked at length about it."

"Will you be moving to Pennsylvania?"

"We plan to stay in Ohio."

"And your future wife is okay with that?"

"More than okay. She suggested it."

"Well, I'll be. She must be quite a person. That's a real sacrifice on her part."

"I know it. It's mainly about Allie. Anna doesn't want to have the poor boppli suffer more than she has."

"I see."

"Since we've made the decision—"

"Have you asked the Lord?"

"Many times."

Tim continued to nod as he stroked his beard. "Well if the gut Lord is in favor of it, who am I to put a damper on it? When were you thinking of getting married? Season's over."

"I was hoping, under the circumstances, we could

marry end of March or early April. No sense holding off till next year. We're too far apart to be traipsing back and forth every week-end."

"Planning a big shindig?"

"Nee. Just the opposite. Since we've both lost mates, we just want a simple ceremony with close family."

Tim chuckled. "We Amish have *really big* close families."

"Only our immediate family. No cousins, well, except for Naomi's kinner. They're like my own kids and maybe Anna will want to invite some close relatives."

"I'll check with the district deacon once you settle on a date. Your fiancé will need the paperwork in our hands soon."

"Jah, she's taking care of it."

"No problem with her standing in her church?"

"I'm sure there's not. She's a God-fearing woman of high morals."

Tim nodded. "I'm sure she is. You wouldn't be wantin' to marry her if she weren't."

"That's for certain," Abe said, relieved to be getting the details worked out. "How about if we say the first Thursday of April. I'm gonna be talking by phone to Anna tomorrow, so if it doesn't work out for her, I'll run by to tell you. I'd like to get things rolling."

Tim removed a small notebook from his vest pocket and turned to the middle. "Looks like a gut day. Nothing on my calendar."

"Gut. Well, I'd better get back to the kinner. Naomi has a quilting bee at her house later. I'm sure she's all a-fussing to get things right."

"Hazel was thinkin' about going but even her mudder can't handle all those maedel."

"She could bring them with her."

"Oh, I don't think so. They sure wouldn't get much sewing done."

Tim walked Abe out to his buggy and patted his horse, Mickey, on the neck. "That's a fine horse you got, Abe. If you ever want to sell him, let me know."

"I'm afraid I'll never sell him. It was Mary's favorite driver. He wasn't acting right the day she had the accident and she took Fervor instead. Maybe if she'd had Mickey…"

Tim placed his hand on Abe's shoulder. "Don't torment yourself, Abe. Gott has things under control. Mary's in a far better place now. We can't ask why."

"I guess not. There aren't any answers, are there? Well, I'll stop by once I speak to Anna."

"Abe, I hope you're doing the right thing. I know you're a young man yet and you could sure use a wife and mudder for them kids. Don't expect things to be real smooth in the beginning. You have lots of relationships which will have to be formed. Sometimes it takes time for kinner to adjust. Pray for patience."

"Denki. I will. I have been already. I believe if the Lord wants it to work, it will."

Tim smiled and nodded. "First Thursday in April. Sounds gut. I'll pray we don't get snow." He winked and Abe grinned back.

"I don't care if it hails golf balls. We're gonna make the best of our situation."

As he pulled away, he pictured telling Anna he'd set the date already. He just hoped she'd be as happy as he was at that moment. He finally admitted to himself how lonely he'd been.

Chapter Twenty-Four

Josiah dried the last of the pots soiled from the night before and placed them in his cabinet below the sink. It was a tussle to get them all in alongside cleaning supplies. Sure was a tiny kitchen, he thought as he wiped out the sink with cleanser. It looked a whole lot better after that. A bachelor doesn't care much about keeping order—at least he hadn't until now. With Beth returning to her job he wanted to impress her with his cleanliness.

He glanced over at his wind-up clock on the small table. She should be here any minute. Yesterday had been a strain. Things were awkward at first, but they were separated by a wall most of the day. Business was slow, so Beth caught up on the paper work, which had been all but ignored in her absence. After cleaning up the kitchen, he put the pot on for coffee and went to check the front. It was spotless. Those annoying cobwebs had disappeared and he smiled when he saw that

Beth had also wiped down the shelving and tops of the display cases. She was amazing. In every way.

He scolded himself for the feelings he still had for this woman. It was obvious they'd never be anything more than employer-employee. Well, maybe friends in time, but marriage? There was no way they could ignite the feelings they had. Was there?

Several buggies passed by before he spotted Beth's trotting quickly down the road. She turned into his parking area and he went outside, forgetting to put on his jacket, and helped her with the unharnessing. After releasing her horse to a fenced-in pasture behind the store, they walked together towards the backdoor.

"Aren't you cold?" she asked as they walked.

"A little bit. I can't wait till it warms up more."

"Jah, spring should keep you busy. Everyone likes to do home improvement when winter's over."

"I can't really handle much more work right now. Not till I get help in the workshop."

"I can help when it's slow," she said as he opened the door and waited for her to go in.

"That would be gut. I appreciate it," he said as he entered the warm kitchen and closed the door behind him.

"I smell kaffi," she said removing her shawl. "And look at this kitchen!" She turned totally around to view the whole room. "You redded up real gut," she said with a grin.

"Well, it was even too much for this old bachelor. It was bad when I didn't have a single clean plate or spoon."

She laughed and headed for the front. "Call me

when the kaffi is ready. I'll drink it in the showroom so I can work at the same time."

"Sure. I'll bring you a cup when it's done. Still use two sugars?"

Her brows rose. "You remember. Jah, two is fine. No cream."

He stood over the pot, timing the brewing process. He could start sanding, but he wasn't ready. Beth still had a strong effect on him. He couldn't deny it. He looked through the window in the door between them. She was sorting through papers totally unaware of his presence. Such a beautiful woman. She was different from all the other Amish women he'd known. So spunky. He loved her intellect—her curiosity—everything about her. Oh, if it had only worked out. He tried to resign himself to remaining single. He certainly could afford a wife. In the short time he'd been in business, he'd already saved over four thousand dollars. When he caught up with the jobs he was working on, he'd have another thirty thousand dollars in the bank. It might be prudent to look for a small house to buy. No woman would be interested in living in his present home, now that more than half of it had been turned into his business.

When the coffee was finished, he set two mugs on a tray he'd picked up at a garage sale and added two cookies he'd been given by a lady from church, who happened to have a daughter of marriage age. Poor girl had eaten more than her share of her mother's baked goods and her chances of attracting a beau were slim.

He pushed the door open and balanced the tray over to the counter where Beth was straightening magazines and catalogs.

"Thought I'd join you before getting back to sanding. I hate that job."

"I'll help. Looks like it's going to be slow today. It started raining."

He followed her eyes to the picture window and nodded. "Jah, at least it isn't snow."

"You're right there. I've had enough snow for a lifetime."

She took her mug and set it on the counter, continuing the job she'd started.

"You don't have to work during coffee break," he said quietly, disappointed at her actions. He'd hoped they'd have a few minutes to converse. He was anxious to tell her about his translation of one of his Greek books.

"It's okay," she responded. "I like to have everything in order before customers come in. A little compulsive I guess." She smiled over.

He thought his heart would melt. Those eyes. Fawn brown, slightly almond shaped. Beautiful.

"Oh, jah." He cleared his throat.

She looked over at him and set her mug down and went over to the seating area. "I guess we have some time."

He followed her over with the tray holding the cookies and his own mug. "A little, I'm sure," he added as he set it on a coffee table. Then he sat in a wooden maple captain's chair he'd made when he was much younger. "I've been working on my Greek."

"Oh gut. What are you translating now?"

"Homer's Iliad. It's a challenge."

"Do you have the English in case you get stuck?" Beth asked.

"Jah, in the back of the book. I confess to cheating more than once."

"Well you haven't been doing it that long. I'm not surprised. Is it as hard as it looks?"

"Mmm. Maybe harder, but I'm determined."

"What would the bishop think about all this?"

"Goodness, I have no idea. I don't think it's wrong, do you?"

Anna laughed and cocked her head to the side. "What I think and what our bishop thinks are two different things—at least on some issues."

"He's pretty strict. Think I should run it by him?"

"I don't know. I see nothing wrong with wanting to learn a language."

"Want me to teach you what I know?"

"Nee. I wouldn't be gut at it. I'm still trying to improve my quilting."

"Ah! So you are a true Amish woman."

She spread her arms. "Every inch of me."

He had to hide his grin, as he tried to get his mind off her comment. "Well, if you change your mind, let me know. What's going on with Anna?"

"Well, I told you she plans to live in Ohio after they marry, right?"

"Jah. That's going to be hard on you and your parents."

Beth looked down at her mug and turned the handle. "Jah, it is. She doesn't want Abe's dochder to have to make the move. The maed is very close to her aenti, who lives next door."

"Didn't you say she lives there?"

"Jah, she does for now. It's Anna's hope that once

she's married to Abe, she can gain the child's trust and she'll move back home."

"That's probably one reason for Abe to remarry."

"Perhaps, though he told Anna he's falling in love with her."

"That's wonderful-gut. And maybe down the road, Anna will feel the same."

"Maybe. I hope so."

"Jah, everyone needs to be loved." He looked down at the plate and reached for a cookie. He didn't want to look at her. He feared what he might say next.

"I guess so. I'm glad I have a gut family."

"Do you plan to marry someday?"

She looked up and her eyes widened. "Funny thing to ask after all we've been through."

"I'm sorry. I take back the question."

"I think you'd better. You promised to keep this all business."

"And if that's what you want, I will honor my promise."

"Okay. I didn't mean to sound angry. I have emotions too, Josiah. You have to consider my feelings."

"I'm sorry, Beth. You're absolutely right. Forgive me?"

"Jah. I'm Amish, remember? What choice do I have?"

He laughed and stood up to leave. "I guess I'd better get back to work. Oh, by the way, what will become of Anna's home?"

"She thinks she'll sell off the house and a couple acres and our bruder will give her something for the rest of the land. He can sure use it."

"I see. That sounds like a gut idea. Does Abe have much land?"

"He has about three hundred acres. He raises steer on part of it. He also has a few dairy cows."

"I'm glad for your schwester."

"She'll be here around noon. Remember? She expects a call from Abe. You said it would be okay."

"Of course it's okay. I just forgot, is all."

"There I go again. I don't know why my nerves are all uppity."

"Probably because of the wedding. The move."

"Possibly. I'm not looking forward to it. She's getting married here, you know."

"Am I invited?"

"I honestly don't know. I haven't talked much to Anna about it. I know it will be small."

"I understand."

"She's asked me to be her *newehocker*. She'll probably ask one more maed to be a side-sitter even though it's not going to be a big wedding. Tradition, I guess."

"That's nice."

"I guess so. It's the fourth time for me to be an attendant."

"And you—nee, I'm not going there."

First she glared and then she broke into laughter. "I have you walking on hot coals, ain't?"

He smiled over and nodded. "I'll stick to business. We'll talk wood and cabinets from now on."

"Jah, that's safer."

Around noon, Anna appeared in order to wait for her phone call. Josiah showed her through his workshop and answered her questions, which were many.

"I'm happy for you, Anna," he said as they walked back to the showroom.

Just then the phone rang. It was exactly twelve o'clock. Anna's smile was radiant and it wasn't lost on Beth, who walked back to the shop area to allow her sister privacy. A stab of jealousy ran through her. Then she thought of all her poor sister had been through and asked the Lord to forgive her sin.

Beth picked up some fine sandpaper and Josiah showed her where to sand. She was silent.

A few minutes later, Anna came through the door, beaming. "He set the date for the first Thursday of April."

"Oh my goodness, That's right around the corner," Beth said.

"Jah, but that's all right. We're not making a big fuss, you know. Josiah, we want you to come though."

"Denki, but I understand you're just having family. Close family."

"Well, we'll probably have a few friends, too. I'm sure my schwester would be upset if you weren't invited," she said with a side-glance at Beth. She felt the glare—it was that strong.

Josiah was amused and winked at Beth, who turned her back to prevent them from seeing her grin. Nothing subtle about Anna, she thought.

"I have to leave now," Anna said as she reached for her shawl. "The buwe are acting up something fierce today. Mamm is watching them and I don't want her to have to put up with their shenanigans."

"Hopefully, they'll be gut for Abe after you're married," Josiah said.

"Poor man. I don't think he knows what he's getting into," Beth stated.

"It's mainly Luke. He's against the marriage and of course, the move."

"He just has to accept it," Beth said, folding her arms.

"Jah, well. Best be going. Mamm and Daed are going to stay for dinner. We're having pot roast."

"Yum. I'll be home regular time tonight. Are you eating the dinner at noon?"

"Jah, as always. We'll save some for you though, Beth."

"You'd better. That's my favorite meal."

Anna looked over at Josiah. "We'll put some aside for you, too, Josiah. Beth can bring it in tomorrow for your lunch."

"Denki. I never turn down gut food. I'm not much of a cook."

"I'm surprised the single Amish maedel aren't flocking at your door. A nice Amish man like you."

Beth noted a flush travel up his neck. "You're embarrassing him, Anna."

"Oh sorry," she said as she giggled. "See you later, Beth."

"Jah."

After she left, Beth returned to the desk just as a young couple entered. Josiah went back to the workshop. Beth enjoyed her salesman's hat the most. She liked talking to strangers. She learned a lot about the world and though she'd never leave her Amish roots, she liked to know what the rest of the population was thinking and doing.

* * *

Josiah looked out as she showed the customers the different cabinets. *Oh, Beth, I still love you. I wish it was us getting married.* He took a deep breath and tried to concentrate on his work.

Chapter Twenty-Five

Almost a week had passed since Abe had spoken with Anna. He was surprised at how often his thoughts turned to the lovely woman who would soon be his wife. He often pictured her shy smile and found himself thinking about her living in his home. Mary's home. But Mary would want him to find someone for their children. That was the kind of woman she had been. He no longer felt heavy guilt about re-marrying. It was now time.

Tomorrow he'd speak to Anna again. The week had gone quickly. He and Naomi had removed all of Mary's personal items. Even some of the kitchen tools which had created so many meals for the family. He gave them to a cousin whose daughter was getting married. He knew Anna would bring many of her own things with her. It might make the transition easier for her to be surrounded by the familiar.

They'd discussed a few things the week before, but with the wedding only three weeks away, they didn't plan on seeing each other until then. After the marriage took place, he'd hire someone to move whatever belongings she wanted to his place. She told him she was busy sorting things out every day. The children wanted their toys and sports items. They had their clothing and Anna wanted her own sewing machine, even though Mary had a good one.

"But I know how to use my own," she had said when they discussed it. "I've sewn on it since I was eight years old. I feel like it's a friend."

He had teased her about it, but she stuck to her guns. Naomi's sewing machine was not the quality of Mary's, so she happily agreed to take it.

Her husband knew an Englisher who had a small Ford truck, who offered to take the trip to pick up Anna's things. Of course, Abe would pay him for his time.

Abe came in from one of the fields where he had turned the fresh soil. The temperatures had reached the sixties and it was time to prepare for his crops. The early rye was already planted. His boots were thick with mud and he went over to the pump to take off the worst.

John was sitting on the ground washing marbles in a small wash pan. He looked up as his father came towards him.

"Did you get the stable mucked, Sohn?" Abe asked as he primed the pump handle for water.

"Not yet."

"Then you should wait to clean your marbles. Your chores come first. You know that."

"I didn't feel like it."

"John, that's not sounding like you. You've always been cooperative."

"I guess."

Abe wiped his damp hands on his trousers and knelt down next to his son. "Wanna talk about it?"

"About what?"

"Whatever it is you're upset about."

"I ain't upset."

"Come on, Sohn. It's the wedding, isn't it?"

"I guess."

"We'll have problems sometimes, but in the end it will be nice to have a mudder in the home again."

"She ain't Mamm."

Abe picked up one of the large boulders and moved it around on his palm. "We've been through this, John. It's time to get over it and accept it."

"I don't like Luke. He's dumb acting."

Abe held back a smile. "Well, maybe he thinks you're the same."

John looked into his father's eyes. "Are you gonna love him more than me?"

"Oh, Sohn." He wrapped his arms around his eldest boy and held him close to his chest. He could feel the boy's chest rising and falling as he tried unsuccessfully to stop the tears.

"I miss her, Daed. And Ruthie, and Bobby and Harvey. I miss them real bad. And things are gonna be even more different when you get married. Maybe I'm scared you'll like Anna's kinner more than us."

"Look, John. I'll never stop loving you or Benny or Allie. Never. I want to learn to love Anna's kinner, too. Love isn't divisible. You can love a whole bunch of people. It's not like it's limited. Understand?"

He nodded and moved slightly away from his father. "I guess so. I don't wanna talk about it anymore."

Abe set the marble back in the pile. "You can finish this up before you do the stable."

"Okay." John sniffed and wiped his arm over his eyes. "I guess I'm being a boppli, ain't."

"Nee. Of course you have doubts about this whole thing. In time, you and Luke will come to grips about this marriage. He's probably struggling just like you are—having a new dat."

"Jah, maybe. He's a pretty gut catcher, anyway."

Abe smiled at his son. "See? You have something in common already. Anna says he's a gut fisherman, too. Maybe you can take him to our fishing hole in the spring." Abe stood and stretched. "Lots more to do today. Spring sure is a busy time."

"Are you gonna go see Anna again before you marry her?"

"I don't think it will happen. We don't have much time and I have a lot of work to finish up while the weather holds."

"Maybe I'm glad. I'll try to like everyone, Daed. Really."

Abe reached over and patted his head. "You're a gut bu, John. It would mean a lot to me if you'd attempt it."

For the first time all day, Abe's son smiled up at him. "I bet I catch bigger fish than Luke."

Abe laughed out loud. "Well, we'll need all the fish we can get to feed our big family. I'll take the little along with big."

Abe went up the walkway to the house. He had prayer to offer up. The rest of the field would have to wait.

* * *

Two weeks before the wedding, Anna sat and had coffee with her mother and sister one Saturday. Sometimes Beth worked on Saturday, but she asked off this week so she could help her sister prepare for her move. The women had been working all morning at Anna's home, packing up small articles which Anna wanted to take with her. Most were from her kitchen.

"It wonders me about the dishes. Should I take them in case Abe doesn't have enough?"

Rose looked over at Anna. "I imagine he does, but you can ask him next time you talk to him."

"I'll have to write notes to myself. Every time we talk I forget something I wanted to ask him. I'm getting real fidgety about this thing."

"Not changing your mind, are you?" Beth asked her sister.

"I'm nervous is all."

"I understand," her mother said, nodding. "It ain't easy to change your whole life like this."

Anna put her head in her hands and tried successfully to control her tears.

"Honey, you'll be real happy. I know it," her mother said as she reached across the table and patted one arm.

"I hope so. I'm gonna miss my family so much. I wish now I hadn't said I'd move. Allie would have come around. I know it."

"You did a very nice thing, Anna. Gott will bless you for your unselfishness."

Beth plunked her mug on the table with a thud. "Maybe Abe was being selfish."

Anna put her arms down and looked over at her sister. "Nee, he was willing to come here. It was me who almost insisted on settling in Ohio. Truthfully, I don't like all the memories this house has for me anyway. The thought of having another man living here in Jeremiah's house was more than I could bear."

"Do you think you'll have a problem living in his wife's home?" Rose asked.

"I don't know."

"Hopefully, Abe will get rid of her clothing and stuff," Beth stated.

"He and Naomi have been working on that. It will be best for everyone."

"And the buwe?" Rose asked, reaching for a brownie, fresh from the oven. "How are they doing?"

"Bad as ever, but I think Luke's the only one who could be a real problem. I've talked with him a dozen times. I just hope some of it sank in."

"He's just a bu. Don't expect much," Beth said.

"On another topic, have you decided about your dress, Anna?" Rose asked. "Your schwester will need to wear the same color."

"I have enough blue fabric left-over from a dress I made last year, to sew up another one for Beth," Anna said. "I pinned it up last night."

"I can help sew it. Who's going to be your other side-sitter?" Beth asked.

"I asked Priscilla Detweiller."

"She's my age," Beth said, surprised.

"But her schwester, Molly, is my age. I've known the family all my life."

"Jah, she's a gut choice, Anna. Nice family."

"Is the mother of the bride gonna sew herself a new frack?" Beth asked her mother.

"I guess I should. I'm getting lazy I'm afraid. After

all, I already have a nice black dress from the last wedding. Do you need a new frack for Rachel?"

"My goodness! I hadn't thought of that. She's outgrowing her church frack."

"I'll have time, Anna," her mother reassured her. "I'll sew it up. Just have me measure her up before we leave later."

"She'll be thrilled. Denki, Mamm. It would help me a lot."

"How many people have you asked to the wedding, Mamm?" Beth asked as she reached for a second brownie.

"Goodness, I'm not sure. I'm thinking about thirty. That ain't many for an Amish wedding."

"It's plenty," Anna said. "Don't forget, Abe will be bringing his family, too."

"Well, maybe I'll invite a couple of your aenties. The ones who cook the best," she added, grinning at her girls.

"I just don't want to end up with a hundred guests," Anna said.

"When I get married, I'm gonna elope and eliminate all that," Beth said. She poured another cup of coffee into her mug. "Anyone else?" she asked, holding the pot in the air.

They both shook their heads. "Save the rest for your daed. He likes it strong."

"I haven't seen him all morning."

"It's spring. I feel like a widow myself till the planting's done. When he hears the dinner bell, he'll be in, quick as a hare."

"That's what I'm cooking," Anna said with a laugh. "Rabbit stew."

"I thought that's what I smelled," Beth said.

"So is Josiah coming to the wedding?" Anna asked.

"I guess so. You asked him. Why did you do that any way? You know we're finished as a couple."

"Truthfully, I'm not sure. I notice he stares at you when you're not looking. I think he still has a case on you."

"No way. Not after the glove incident. It's over between us. I wish you hadn't invited him. I don't want him to get the wrong idea."

"What, that you might still care?"

Rose looked from one daughter to the other and back again. "I'll miss these pleasant little battles you two have when you're together."

They both stared at her. "Mamm, we aren't fighting," Anna said, alarmed.

"Well, you could sure fool your mudder. Anna, don't pry into Beth's mind. She'll tell us when she has something important to say. In the meantime, she works for the man. She needs the money, so maybe it's better this way."

Beth's mouth dropped open. "Really? Coming out of my mudder's mouth!" She grinned over at Rose. "You're the matchmaker, Mamm."

"I've given up on you, Beth. It's in Gott's hands. I'm staying out of it."

Beth let out an exaggerated sigh of relief. "Too bad the Amish don't have nuns. I'd make a great one."

Anna laughed and shook her head. "I doubt that. Somewhere there's a man just perfect for you. I just think you haven't met him yet."

"Let's get back to work," Beth said. "I should stop by the shop and see if Josiah needs help."

"See, Anna?" Rose began, "Your schwester doesn't care about him at all." She winked at Anna and they returned to their packing.

Chapter Twenty-Six

Abe made arrangements to rent a small bus with a driver for the wedding guests. His parents, two sisters, twin brothers with their families, plus his brother Sam, were all planning to come to the wedding. With thirteen children, not counting his own, the bus would be filled. Abe's aunt offered to care for his grandmother who had Alzheimer's. He counted twenty-seven family members headed to Pennsylvania. Not a bad showing, considering. He'd asked Mary's family to come too, but they declined. He realized it might be too difficult for them and suggested they meet Anna and her children once they return.

Naomi was busy sewing up clothes for the kinner. Abe bought his black suit and bowtie from a local store and purchased a fresh white shirt and a new black-rimmed hat for the occasion. He also bought new hats for his boys. Excitement was taking the place of apprehension as he got closer to the big day. The last time he talked to Anna he detected a giddiness in her voice. She was probably nervous. He'd try to make it as easy as possible for her to adjust to his family and her new home.

John seemed to be adjusting to the idea of the marriage and even straightened his room in preparation for a roommate.

A week before the wedding, Abe was in the kitchen with his sister sorting through the cabinets to make room for some of Anna's things. The boys were checking their board games and puzzles, eliminating the ones with missing pieces. Anna had mentioned her children would be bringing a couple of new games with them. Allie sat on a rocker with her eight-year-old cousin Emmy, looking bewildered. She chewed on her blanket and held onto Emmy's kapp strings.

Benny talked non-stop about Anna's boys and made a list of things he was going to show them. "They'll love my treehouse, won't they, Daed?"

"I'm sure they will," Abe said.

"They'll probably be too scared to climb it," John said, his mouth drooped into a frown.

"Not Mark or Matthew. They're not scared of anything."

"Oh, right," John said.

"Buwe, what have I told you about arguing? It has no place in this household."

There was silence temporarily, then Benny talked about wanting a party with just children his age so Anna's boys could make friends.

"That's a nice idea," his Aunt Naomi said, smiling over. "We can do it at our place if you want."

"Jah, you make gut cake."

"So does Anna," John said, unexpectedly.

Abe looked over at Naomi. "Jah, that's for sure," he said holding back a chuckle.

"That doesn't mean I want her for a mamm," John said quickly.

"She's nice, John," Benny said. "And she'll like Allie. Maybe she'll come back to live with us, huh, Daed?"

"That's the plan."

"Abe, what about all the chipped cups and mugs? Should be get rid of them?" Naomi asked as she reached on the upper shelf for the strange assortment of mugs.

"I guess so. And some of my pots have broken handles. Anna's going to replace those too. I told her about them."

"She may want her own dishes."

"Jah, we can wait on that one. We may need them all with a growing family. Besides, these Corelle plates last forever and still look fine."

The children were back in the sitting room now and Emmy was organizing a card game while Allie played with blocks.

"Bruder, I don't mean to get personal, but are you and Anna going to add to the family?"

"I hope so, in time. It's not like the first time you marry. We're not in any hurry."

"I see. Of course not. I shouldn't have asked." She moved the filled carton and set a fresh empty one on a chair to be filled.

"I hope we'll have more kinner eventually, though."

"You're both still young. It might be gut for the family. Kind of tie it all together."

"Jah. Anna and I haven't talked much about all that.

It seemed way too early. We may have separate bedrooms in the beginning. I'll leave it up to her."

"You won't have a separate bedroom, not with eight kinner," she reminded him.

He nodded. "There's always the sofa."

Naomi stopped wrapping the damaged mugs and looked over at her brother. "Is that what you want?"

"I don't know. Probably not, but I'm thinking of Anna."

"Maybe she needs to be near you as well, Bruder. I'm sure she's missed being close to someone."

"You're getting out of your territory," he said, smiling.

"I'm sorry. I'll stay out of it."

"I'm not upset, it's just that we're both still suffering from our losses. We're praying about it and we'll let the Lord direct us."

"Gut. Now we should go through the utility room. I'm sure there are outgrown boots we can give away or store."

Beth had customers most of the morning. When she marked the wall calendar, she realized it was just one week from the wedding. The clothing was finished and there was little to do except clean, which was on the agenda for the week-end. Her parents had already started. The barn was going to be used so Isaiah and Zach were working to clean it up. Rose's three sisters were helping in the house. Weddings demanded a lot of preparation and though they didn't expect many guests, the work load was almost the same. The benches and tables would be brought in and set up ahead of time. They'd add a few extras on the wedding day in case more people showed up unexpectedly. Since everyone in the district was aware of the wedding to take place and the circumstances, it was probable that more guests would arrive.

While Beth was finishing up an order with a customer, a tall, thin, dark-haired Amish man about Josiah's age came in and stood watching from a corner of the room. He twirled his straw hat in his hands as he watched her. After the customer left, she asked if she could help him.

"I'm here to see Josiah Yoder. For the job."

"Oh, I didn't realize he'd placed an ad."

"I heard about it from a friend. Can he see me?"

"I'll check with him. Have a seat," she suggested, pointing to a small chair. He smiled and nodded.

When she went back to see Josiah, he was using the jigsaw on a piece of trim. He stopped and raised his brows.

"Sorry to interrupt you, Josiah, but there's a man who stopped by for the job."

"Did you get his name?"

"Nee. I didn't think to."

"That's okay. You can tell him to come back. I can stop what I'm doing."

"Do you want me to make kaffi for you both?"

"Nee, that's all right."

When she returned she asked his name. More for her own information at this point.

"It's Daniel King. But my friends call me Shorty."

"But you're so tall," Beth said grinning.

"Jah, that's why they call me Shorty. And your name, Ma'am?"

"It's Beth. Beth Beachy." She debated about extending her hand, but refrained, since some men thought that was forward of a woman. He'd learn soon enough. "Josiah said to come on back. Through the door over there," she said pointing towards the workshop.

"Denki, Beth Beachy."

His wide grin exposed perfectly straight and the whitest of teeth. He was quite handsome and it was not lost on Beth. After he left the showroom, she checked a small mirror on the wall and tucked a loose strand of hair under her kapp.

About an hour later, the two men came into the showroom. "I guess you already met Shorty. He's going to help us out here, starting next Monday."

"Jah, we met all right. *Wilkum* to our happy little shop," Beth said, coquettishly. She glanced over at Josiah, who looked none too pleased.

"Jah well, I guess I'll be going." His neck flushed. "See you at eight on Monday." He nodded towards them both and left the shop.

"Well, that should be a big help to you, Josiah."

"He's had a lot of experience for his age." Josiah pulled on his suspenders and leaned against the wall.

"Is he from around here? I don't recognize him."

"He lives two districts over. I hope it works out." He straightened up and headed towards the back.

"Jah, me too."

"I'm sure you do," he said with a huff as he turned and went through to the shop area.

Beth giggled as she checked the newest order. He must still care a wee bit to get jealous over a simple remark.

At noon, Beth went into the refrigerator for her lunch. She'd made a sausage sandwich and just in case Josiah didn't have food on hand, she'd made an extra one for him. At first he refused it, but once he smelled the fresh-made sausage and onions, he reneged. They sat together silently at first.

"It's gut," he muttered, staring at the wall behind her.

"Oh jah. Daed makes the best."

"So what do you think of our new employee?" he asked.

"Not much to think. I barely know him."

"True. He learned carpentry alongside an uncle."

"How come he's not working for him?"

"Apparently there wasn't enough work for two. He wants to buy property down the road."

"That's wise. It won't get cheaper. That's for sure."

"Jah."

"I'm gonna put on a pot of kaffi, Josiah. I need a pick-me-up."

"Okay. Make me some too then."

"Bitte?"

"Oh jah. Please." While they waited for the pot to boil, Beth poked in her toot for potato chips. She offered some to Josiah, but he shook his head.

"Watching your waistline, Josiah?"

He let out a laugh. "Should I be?"

"Nee. You're fine." She could hear the chips crunch between her teeth. Otherwise there was no sound.

Finally, Josiah broke the silence. "Did Anna tell you I stopped by to see her last evening?"

"Nee. Whatever for?"

"We had business to discuss."

"Okay, stop trying to intrigue me. What business?"

"I'm thinking of buying her home."

"Seriously?"

"Very serious. It's a nice home. Perfect for a large family and the price is right. Of course, I'd have to borrow money from my daed and pay him back over time."

"Was she interested in selling it to you?"

"Why not? My money's as gut as anyone else's."

"But you're only one person."

"I plan to multiply that."

"Have you someone picked out?"

"Nee. Not yet, but there's someone I'm thinking about." He realized he'd have to watch every word from this point forward.

"Do I know the maed?"

"You're not going to get anything further out of me," he said, smiling. "I think the coffee's ready."

"Nee. Not yet. See the color? Needs a bit more brewing." She sat back and folded her arms. "Well, Anna's place is lovely. Any woman would be happy to live there."

"That's what I figured."

"Of course, if she loves you, she'd probably be happy even here." Beth swept the air with her arm.

"It's way too small for a family."

"I'm just saying…" She looked around at the tight kitchen. "Well, maybe you're right. It would be pretty hard to make a meal in here for more than two people."

"The kaffi is almost black. See?" He pointed to the stove and Beth rose and turned it off.

"Better give it a minute to settle. Do you have anything sugary to eat?"

Abe laughed. "You sure have a sweet tooth, Beth."

"I admit it. But I've never had a cavity."

"You have a lovely smile."

"Denki." He was getting personal again. Dare she hope? She took their two mugs out of the cabinet and set them on the table. "So? No goodies?"

"I'm totally out. Sorry."

"It's okay. I'll pack something tomorrow. There're always baked goods in our house."

Their conversation was limited to impersonal discussions of his business, which for the moment was satisfactory.

Beth admitted she liked being back with Josiah. It wasn't just the pay, she enjoyed working outside the home. It was challenging and if she was honest with herself, she liked keeping an eye on Josiah. He might not care anymore, but she still cared—deeply. At least this way, she'd know if another woman entered into his life. Of course, what would she do if one did? She'd cross that bridge when she came to it and hopefully, she never would have to cross it.

Chapter Twenty-Seven

Rose kept wiping her eyes with her apron as she stood by the stove stirring the vegetable soup she'd made for supper. Isaiah turned the page of the Budget and read aloud about friends they knew from Church. "They just had a new boppli," he said, looking over at his wife.

"That's nice," she responded, unenthusiastically.

His brows rose. "Got allergies?"

"Nee."

"A cold?"

"Nee."

"So why are you sniffling up a storm?"

"You should know why," she said, setting the wooden spoon on a plate.

"Anna."

"Jah. I'm dreading the move, Isaiah. It won't be the same with her so far away."

"I know. Could be worse. The Martin's daughter moved to Colorado."

"It can always be worse," she said, slightly irritated.

Isaiah set the paper on the next chair and rose. He went and put his arms around her. "At least we know she's gonna be happy."

"How do we know? We barely know the man. In fact, Anna barely knows him. Maybe he'll beat the kinner!"

"Now, Rose, you're getting carried away. He has a gut character. I can tell about men. He has gentleness."

"Maybe he's pretending. Maybe—"

"Hush now," he said, placing his index finger over her lips. "You're letting your imagination run away with you. Gott forbid, but if it doesn't work out, Anna always has a home with us. She knows that and we'll go visit her often, if that will make it easier on you."

"Promise?"

"Jah, of course. Don't you think it'll be hard on me as well?"

"It's different. You're busier. And if Beth moves…"

"I think that dochder of ours will be here for a long time to come."

"I want her to marry. I'm not hoping she'll be here forever."

"I know. I know. Now stop with the tears. We have to be strong for Anna. She's gonna miss us, too, you know. What she's doing by moving to Ohio is a very unselfish act and we have to support her decision."

"I ain't done anything to change it, though I'd like to."

"She's an adult. She's been through a lot and so has Abe. I believe the gut Lord brought them together."

"I guess you're right. I'm being selfish," Rose said as she wiped her eyes for the last time. "Want to try the soup?"

"Sure. Any fresh bread to go with it?"

"You can have one slice, Isaiah, the rest is for to-night. Anna and the kinner are coming soon. She's cleaned out the refrigerator except for the milk. In two days…"

"Jah, in two days, Abe will be here. So you've got things worked out about his family? Where they're gonna stay?"

She shook her head. "His kinner will stay here. He has several cousins living nearby, so he's taking care of the arrangements for his family. I'm glad, because I have enough to do planning the wedding. I looked out at the barn this morning while you were in the fields. I can't believe how clean you men made it."

"Took a lot of hours and people to get it that way and we'll have to do more the day before the wedding. Jah, Wednesday is gonna be mighty busy for everyone. And she's having a small wedding."

"Hazel Zook is bringing the celery. They grow it in their greenhouse."

"That's nice of her. I guess you'd better invite her then, don't you think?"

"Jah, I already did." Rose reached for two bowls and poured soup into them. "Rachel has been real quiet lately. I think the maed is upset about leaving."

"Jah, you two have been so close. I'm glad he has a little maed for her to play with."

"Me too. She talks about her a lot. I think that's the main reason he's re-marrying. She hasn't been staying with him and his buwe, you know."

"Jah, Beth told me. The maed's so young. She needs a mamm."

"Her aenti has been like a mamm to her. I hope it won't cause conflict."

"Why should it? I understand she has a big family of her own. And they live next door to each other."

"True. I guess it can work out."

"Honey, Gott can make everything work out. They must put their faith in Him, and so must we. Now let's have our soup. Looks like you made enough for a week."

"You're getting it again tonight, Isaiah. Hope you don't get sick of it. I'm just not up to making a roast. We have leftover rye bread for now."

"I can eat your soup every meal if I have to. You're a gut cook, Rosie."

"Denki." He always had a way with words. Unusual for an Amish man of his age, but he was unusual. Rose had been blessed.

Abe worked with Naomi to get things packed up for the wedding.

"Leave your suit on a hanger, Abe. You don't want it all wrinkled."

"The buwe's too, I'm thinking," he added as he hung his suit on a peg in his bedroom. "Gut thing we have family to stay with."

"Jah, it will be fun to see our cousins again. And it's not even a funeral," she said with a grin.

"We'll see more of them maybe after the marriage, since Anna will want to visit her family often."

"I hope it works out for her. You know we'll lend a hand anytime you want to travel."

"Jah, I appreciate that." He walked over to his sister and took her hands in his. "You've been a wonderful-gut schwester, Naomi. I'll never forget all you and William have done for us. I don't think I could have made it without you."

"I'm sure you would have, Abe, but I'm glad we were here to help you. And now you're turning a new chapter in your book."

"Jah. It's a little scary, but I've felt Gott's guidance throughout the whole thing. Even the way we met. It had to be providential."

"And I believe you and Anna are gut for each other. She's very kind and sweet."

"She is. She's a fine woman. I just hope I can be a gut husband and gut father to her kinner."

"You will be. You're a wonderful man." She dropped his hands and surrounded him with her arms. They stood like that for several moments.

"Now don't let me cry. We'll still be neighbors and we'll see each other often," she added as she stood back.

"Jah, thank Gott. What time is the bus coming on Wednesday, do you remember what I told you?"

"You said six in the morning."

"We could leave earlier, although I want to get the milking done and the other animals fed first."

"Best to leave it that way. We all have our chores before we leave. It was nice of our other neighbors to offer to help while we're gone."

"Jah. We hope to come back Saturday, you know."

"William had hoped we'd return Friday, but he agrees that would be difficult. We're all going to help clean up on Friday."

"There shouldn't be much to do. We won't even have a hundred people coming."

"You'd be surprised. Sometimes a few more arrive who you'd forgotten. We ended up with four hundred at our wedding."

"Oh jah, I remember. Mary and I had even more than that." He looked down at his feet. "I have to stop thinking about the past."

"It's hard, bruder—even impossible. Just don't talk to Anna about Mary all the time. It would be hurtful to a new bride."

He nodded. "We've talked at length about our past marriages. There isn't much more to say."

Naomi folded his extra shirts carefully and placed them in his suitcase. "And now I have to go pack for us. My kinner are so excited."

"So are mine, except for John. He's doing better, but he still walks around with a frown most of the time."

"That will change when he gets to know Anna's kinner better. Luke and he will be best friends some-day. Mark my words."

"I pray you're right. Okay, on to the buwe's rooms. I can handle it if you want to get back home."

"Jah, Allie should be up from her nap soon. See you later," she added as she made her way down the stairs and to her home next door.

That night as Abe knelt in prayer, he asked the Lord for a safe trip to Pennsylvania. Then he asked for bless-ings on each of his family and Anna's as well. His heart was beating quickly as he thought about the coming marriage.

"Lord, help me to be a gut dat for Anna's kinner as well as my own. Give me patience. I know it ain't gonna be easy blending our two families, but I also know that with you helping, it can work out just fine. And help me be patient about Anna, too. I think it's harder for a man to wait for certain things than for a woman. She's a very desirable lady and sometimes I want to grab her and kiss her, but I need to show restraint. Please help me with this. Let me know when she's ready to be close to me and share my bed. I never want to offend her in any way.

"And Allie—help her to love Anna and her kinner and want to come home real soon to be part of our family. It breaks my heart to have her living away from us, even if it is just next door. Bless Naomi and William and all their kinner. Denki for providing people for me through these past months who helped me through my terrible painful days. I hope my Mary and my dear kinner are happy in Heaven with You, Lord. I bet little Harvey is climbing the biggest trees. He had no fear." His eyes began to water as he named his children and spoke of them to God.

"And Lord, lastly, help me to get over all the pain so I can be a gut mate and dat for Anna and her family. It's so hard sometimes, but I feel your presence in my life. Denki."

He remained on his knees for several minutes, basking in the peace only the Lord gives. Finally, he rose and laid on his bed. A few moments later, he was sound asleep. His gentle snores eked through the walls and comforted his buwe, who were anxiously awaiting the trip. All but John who laid awake until midnight.

Chapter Twenty-Eight

Anna paced up and down the drive expecting Abe and his family to arrive at any moment. It was nearly seven in the evening. They'd probably stopped for meals and bathroom breaks, but she'd hoped they'd be here by now. So many details to go over before the big day. Goodness, the big day was tomorrow! Her stomach twisted ruthlessly in her body. Excitement and apprehension fought for space in her mind as she visualized their ceremony.

Beth and her parents had just left for home and the children were busy blowing up balloons for the big event. She could hear them arguing as to who had the most balloons, but she tuned it out. They'd just have to work it out amongst themselves. She had too much on her mind.

At last, she heard the bus arrive. It turned down her drive and she moved back to allow the driver to park in the parking area. Benny was sitting in the front seat by the window and grinned at her with his big beautiful smile. He sure looked like his father. Then she saw Abe lean over to wave. Oh, he was a fine looking man. What a dear smile.

As everyone climbed out, her boys came running out of the house, with Rachel taking up the rear.

Benny jumped up and down from excitement and then he and Matthew and Mark went back to the bus to help carry in their luggage.

After Abe's family greeted Anna and the kinner, she invited them into the house. "I've made lemon sponge pies and I have kaffi made already."

Abe's mother, Agnes, gave Anna a tender hug. "You must be getting excited," she said as she stepped back and held Anna's shoulders briefly.

"Jah and a little nervous."

"To be expected. Your little ones seem real excited, too."

"Jah. For certain. I hope they calm down soon."

Abe's father came over and nodded. "That pie sounds like a gut idea. I could go for something home-made. The place we stopped for supper was pretty bad."

"Now, Timothy, it filled us up. That's all that mattered at that point."

Abe's sister with Down's syndrome gave Anna a hug. "You will be pretty, Anna. The prettiest bride ever," she said, her eyes gleaming.

"That's very nice of you to say, Eve. Do you like lemon sponge pie, too?"

"It's my favorite, I think. Is it, Mamm?" she asked turning to her mother, who nodded back.

"One of your favorites, Eve dear."

Naomi walked over with Allie in her arms. The

child turned and buried her head into her aunt's shoulder, refusing to look over even when Abe patted her back. "It's okay, Allie. Anna just wants to say hullo."

Allie was adamant. She shook her head without moving away from Naomi. "She'll be okay soon," Naomi said. "She's pretty shy and it was a long trip. I think she's tired."

"Didn't she nap at all?" Abe asked as they stood waiting for the rest of the family to emerge from the bus. They were collecting some trash to dispose of and the driver asked to use the bathroom.

"Actually, she slept for a couple hours."

Abe's brothers and their wives and families came over to greet Anna and the children. Some of the older children began throwing a ball around in the yard. It was nearly dark now and they kept mislaying the ball in the darkening grasses. Finally, they turned and headed towards the house. His family followed.

"We can't stay long," his mother said. "Our cousins are expecting us and they go to bed early."

"I understand," Anna said, relieved that there would soon be time for her and Abe to be by themselves.

Sam, Abe's single brother was the last to get off the bus. He kissed Anna lightly on her cheek and patted her boys on the head. Then he tickled Rachel who giggled and ran in the house. There was such excitement in the air.

After about an hour, the family left for their relative's homes. "We'll be back by seven tomorrow, Abe," his father called out as they headed down the path. "Big day. Try to get some sleep everyone."

"It's not going to be easy," Anna said under her breath to Abe who was standing next to her. He reached for her hand. After everyone was on board, with the exception of his children, Abe and Anna headed back into the house.

"I'll be glad when it's over and we can start our life together," Abe said.

"Me too. Too bad we can't leave Friday, but I wouldn't want to leave all that work for my family."

"Of course not. It's only one more day." He squeezed her hand and she stopped and looked up into his eyes.

"Are you sure you want to do this?"

"Seriously? You're asking me now?" He said grinning. "Of course, I'm sure. You're not changing your mind, are you?"

She shook her head. "Nee. I'm getting really excited, Abe. But just a wee bit nervous."

"Of course. Gut thing it's going to be a small wedding."

"Jah, it is. We have family picnics bigger than this. Do you think Allie has any idea of what's going on?"

"Not really. She's been more timid than usual though. She knows something's happening."

"Poor maed. It may be a few days after we're back in Ohio before she will come stay with us."

"Jah, I expect that to be true. But surely by the end of April we'll be a complete family again."

"That should be our goal, Abe."

He nodded as they began walking towards the back door to the kitchen. John was sitting at the table reading a book about baseball which he'd brought with him. Luke was nowhere in sight. The rest of the children were in the front sitting room and there was laughter along with loud voices as they played together.

"Don't you want to help blow up balloons?" Anna asked Abe's eldest boy.

John shook his head. "They have enough people doing that. I just want to read."

"Where's Luke?" she asked.

He shrugged. "I don't know. I think he went to his room."

"You'll be sleeping with him, John. Want me to show you where his room is?"

"I remember. Last one on the right."

"Can I get you anything else to eat?" Anna asked the sad-looking boy.

"No thanks. Your pie was gut though."

"Denki. I'm glad you liked it."

"Luke, where did you put your clothes?" Abe asked.

"In the other room."

"Why don't you take them upstairs and get them out of the way."

It looked as if there would be an objection, but then Luke rose and nodded as he went to get them. "Okay."

They were alone. For a brief moment, they were alone. Abe drew Anna close to him and lifted her chin. She closed her eyes as he bent to kiss her lips. Suddenly, Rachel charged into the room. He stepped back quickly and Anna leaned over to see why her daughter was in tears.

"Mark grabbed my last balloon and he won't let me have it. It's not fair."

Anna looked over her daughter's head to Abe, who smiled at her. "Well, I'll go speak to your bruder. I may have other balloons somewhere."

"My breath is almost all wore out, Mamm. This was gonna be my last and bestest one."

When she returned, Abe was at the sink, washing out used glasses.

"Abe, you don't have to do that," she said, amazed to see a man behind the sink.

"I'm kinda used to kitchen detail, Anna. I really don't mind."

"Does that mean I have to till the fields?" she asked with her head cocked to the side.

He laughed as he set the washrag to the side. "Nope. You'll be quite busy enough with our brood."

"Oh jah, you can say that again."

"I'll be heading over to your bruder's soon, after we get the kinner down for the night. You said he's expecting me?"

"Jah. They thought they'd stay home tonight since we were having your family come by."

"I'm sorry we can't seem to find a minute to be alone."

"Me, too." She blushed as she remembered how close they had come to sharing their first kiss. But then, maybe it was better to wait. After all, they weren't married yet. Was she disappointed? Mmm. Perhaps a wee bit. He had a nice minty smell to his breath and his arms had felt rather special around her. Maybe it wouldn't be many weeks before she could allow herself to submit to his embraces. It seemed like a long, long time since she'd been close to a man. And she was a young woman with desires like any woman her age, though through her grief she'd forgotten what it was like to be cherished and intimate.

After the children finally quieted down for the night, she was going to go next door with Abe, but he insisted on going alone. "I don't want you to walk alone in the dark," he said as they heard a knock on the kitchen door. Then her brother Zach popped his head in and entered.

"Hey, there you are, Abe. Figured you were about ready to turn in for the night. I brought my lantern with me. It's pitch black out there now." He turned to his sister. "You look beat, Anna."

"Gee, denki," she said pouting.

"Big day tomorrow. You need your sleep."

Abe patted her shoulder. "See you tomorrow, Anna. I hope you sleep okay."

"I'll be lucky to sleep at all," she said as she walked them to the door.

After they left, she sat at the table to collect her thoughts. It would be a miracle if she slept. Her insides felt like a bundle of ostrich feathers. It certainly was too late to change her mind—not that she really wanted to. She just wanted everything to be over with and to lead a normal life again. After preparing for bed, she tiptoed past the children's rooms. Rachel slept by herself. Good thing Anna had prepared her about Allie going with Naomi to the cousin's house. It was too soon to expect the child to stay in a strange place without her aunt. Rachel's giraffe had fallen to the floor. Anna picked it up and laid it beside her daughter's pillow. She kissed her cheek and moved down the hallway.

The three younger boys were sharing the middle bedroom. Matthew had given his bed to Benny and was sleeping on a bed roll on the floor. He was whistling through his teeth, but it was rhythmic and apparently didn't bother the other two. She smiled as she checked the other boys.

John and Luke shared a room with twin beds on opposite sides of the room. They had their backs turned towards each other, but Anna saw them talking together earlier. It was a start.

She made her way to the bathroom and prepared for the night. Glancing in the mirror, she removed her kapp and untwisted her hair. The golden locks draped past her shoulders, making her appear younger than her thirty years of age. Her spring-green eyes stared back at her and she stood thinking about the next night. They'd be sharing her bedroom. The one she'd occupied as a girl. It would be strange indeed, but there would be no intimacy. She simply couldn't—not yet. At least they would not be in the marital bed she'd shared with her beloved husband.

After brushing her teeth and washing her face and hands, she made her way into her bedroom and pulled down the covers and slid into bed. As she lay staring at the ceiling, she realized there was nearly a full moon casting shadows against the wall. A large bird's shadow startled her as it appeared soaring across the wall. Probably the owl who occupied the oak tree in the front yard. He'd lived there for ages.

What would it be like to live in Ohio? Would her loneliness cast an even larger shadow over her new marriage? If she couldn't adjust, would Abe be willing to relocate to Pennsylvania? But she'd agreed to sell her home to Josiah. He was already arranging for a surveyor for the property. He was quite content with the house and two acres and he agreed to her price without hedging. She might never get such an opportunity again. Plus, it meant her parents would have a good neighbor. Who knows? Maybe someday her sister would share the home with Josiah. She could only hope.

No, this decision was final. She would make the best of her situation. She was fond of Abe and could even envision it being more someday. He was clean, intelligent, a good father, a gentleman and a good worker. On top of that she found him very attractive, and a good listener. What more could she ask for? Jeremiah was never coming back. It was time to close that part of her book for good. Yes, it was time to move on. And with God's help, she would be just fine. Of that, she was certain. Before turning her head to sleep, she prayed the Lord's Prayer. Her stomach was calm now. The feathers were gone. And soon a new day would dawn. *Denki, Gott.*

Chapter Twenty-Nine

Anna was amazed to see the clock by her bed. It was five o'clock and she'd fallen right to sleep the night before in spite of today being her wedding day. She heard footsteps in the hallway and then several sets of feet clambering down the stairway. Rachel knocked on her door and came in when Anna invited her. She and her giraffe joined Anna in bed for cuddling.

"You're gonna get married today, right, Mamm?" the child asked in her raspy morning voice.

"That's right, sweetheart. And you will have a daed again. Is that gut?"

"Yup. And Mr. Giraffe will be happy too. He doesn't like it when I'm sad."

"I'm sure he doesn't, and neither do I."

"Are you gonna smile more, Mamm?"

"I hope so, honey," Anna said as she pulled her even closer and kissed her forehead.

"The buwe are all up already. I heard them talk about going fishing."

"Goodness, there won't be time for that. We have to get over to Grossdawdi's place and prepare for the wedding. Please go tell them they can't go anywhere while I get dressed."

Rachel jumped off the bed and toddled into the hallway. "Hope they listen to me, Mamm. You know how naughty they are."

Anna's heart beat quickly as she pulled on her frack from the day before and twisted her hair into place as she made her way down the stairs. She found the children in the kitchen eating fruit and picking at the pie that was left from the night before. They were talking merrily about their plans. Even John and Luke joined in.

"Buwe, I'm sorry, but your plans to fish won't work out today. We have to go over to my parents' home to help with the wedding preparations."

"Aw, gee, Mamm," Matthew started. "We can't do much there. We can fish real quick and then come over."

"Nee. That won't work," Anna said, her voice stern and hopefully authoritative. "I'll scramble up a dozen eggs—after you buwe check the henhouse. You all need to eat a gut breakfast since it will be awhile before we eat again."

"Jah, weddings go on forever," John said, none too pleased.

"Maybe we can skip it," Luke said.

"There is no way, young man. Now I'm nervous enough without you giving me a hard time. You can help me, Luke. Mark and Benny, check for eggs—and Matthew, feed the chickens. As soon as we're done here, we're going over to help with the wedding."

"I thought you packed your big fry pan," Luke said.

"Oh goodness, you're right. Maybe we'll take the eggs over to grossmammi's and eat there. I don't have any dishes either."

The children laughed and John slapped Luke lightly on the back. "You got out of that one," he said. At first Luke looked like he was being challenged, but when he saw the grin on John's face, his body relaxed and he joined in the laughter.

The wedding clothes were already at Rose's house, so Anna packed up her brush and toiletry articles in a small overnight bag, along with items for the children. As she was gathering her shawl and her boots, Abe appeared at the kitchen door. She motioned for him to let himself in and he came right over to her.

"Hi Anna. How did you sleep?"

"Real gut. I was surprised. And you?"

"Not a wink. I've been up all night. But at least I got a lot of praying done. I think the gut Lord is tired of me praising Him. Are you all ready to go?"

"Just about. The kinner are upstairs gathering their things."

"Did they behave for you?"

"Jah. It's gone pretty gut. I feel like I could kutz though."

He went over to her and put his arms around her. "It will be over with soon and then we can get back to normal."

"Jah, whatever 'normal' means anymore." She smiled up at him. "Excited?"

"Of course. We're doing the right thing, Anna. Gott brought us together for this very day."

"I believe He did, too. I'm sure we'll have a gut marriage."

He moved back but kept her hand in his for an extra moment. Then the children began to gather in the kitchen. Once they were ready, they made their way the quarter-mile by foot. Rachel walked between Abe and Anna holding their hands, and the boys used scooters or walked along beside them. It filled Anna's heart as she saw the children together. It seemed like reassurance from above to watch them interact with each other. Though John and Luke separated themselves somewhat, their body language looked less strained. Abe must have felt the same way, since he grinned over at Anna. "Nice family, ain't?"

She nodded and smiled back.

Zach was already in the barn with his father, sweeping it out for the last time. Abe went to join them along with the boys and a few minutes later his own father and brothers arrived. It wasn't really work with so many hands, and joy filled the air. Weddings were always times of celebration and perhaps this one more than most, due to the circumstances.

Beth and her mother were finishing up potato salad in huge bowls while Naomi and Aunt Ellie were trying to organize the younger children, to not only stay out of the way, but to have projects geared toward the reception. Napkins needed to be folded, plastic cups wiped down, paper plates opened and laid aside—many jobs which the children could handle.

Once that was done, the women joined the others and prepared more dishes. Some extra celery had to be purchased since it was April and it didn't store well forever.

Ellie worked on the creamed celery.

There was a short break and Rose went over to Anna and Beth who were unfolding chairs and setting them around the perimeter of the sitting room. "You maedel have to get ready. I'll get someone else to do that. Quick now, it's getting late. We have to start the ceremony in an hour."

Anna's eyebrows hit her kapp. "Oh my, I didn't realize how late it was. I need to bathe."

"Jah, well, quick like a bunny then," Rose said, tapping her daughter on her back end.

Beth followed behind. "You first, Anna. Then I'll shower. Your clothes are in your old room. That's where you'll be tonight?"

"Jah."

"I figured. Okay. Towels?"

"Mamm put a stack in the bathroom. Where's Abe going to get ready?"

"I think he just went back to Zach's. I can't keep track of everyone. Goodness, it's a gut thing we're having a *small* wedding."

"Jah? Not so small!" Beth was looking out the front window of the bathroom. "Look!"

Anna moved next to her and stared, mouth agape, as buggy after buggy turned into their drive and headed towards the grassy area in the back. She counted fourteen buggies and there were more behind them!

"Mercy! We didn't invite all those people! Where are they coming from?"

"I guess when your intentions were published, they just figured you'd want everyone there!"

"Oh, what will we do? We won't have enough food or tables or—"

Beth turned and grabbed her hands. "Anna, you forget we're Amish. There is always enough food. I'm sure every single buggy is jammed with casseroles and cakes. And as far as tables and benches? The deacon left extras—just in case. Guess he figured it might happen."

"So much for a private little wedding," Anna said, finding it difficult to swallow.

"Amish don't allow small weddings," Beth chuckled.

"I hope Abe won't be upset."

"Dear Schwester, you can find a way to worry about everything. Relax and enjoy the attention. This is the beginning of your new life."

Anna embraced Beth and held her tightly. "I'm going to miss you so much."

"Now we don't have time for tears," she choked back, as she held Anna in a yet firmer embrace. Then their tears turned to laughter as they released their holds. Tears were streaming down both their smiling faces. How many emotions wrapped together on such a day as this.

As Anna washed her long blonde curls, she pictured Abe. What would he think of her when she was out of her Amish persona and just a woman? Hopefully, he wouldn't be disappointed in her. As the suds vanished and her hair squeaked from cleanliness, she finished her showering and wrapped herself up in her towel, which was worn from years of use. She'd be leaving all that was familiar. Everything took on special meaning as she used things for the last time, for a while anyway. Not forever. They would return. Abe had promised that. But surely, it couldn't be too often. Farming didn't allow for huge breaks of time, not dairy and cattle, anyway. Thankfully, family often pitched in to allow times of escape.

After Beth showered, she dressed quickly and went in to help Anna pin her apron over her new frock. Then she offered to braid her sister's hair for her.

As Anna sat on the edge of the bed, her head turned towards her sister, she thought of the many times they had shared this time to chatter on about their daily lives. A chapter all but closed.

"Ouch. You still pull too hard," she said to Beth, a smile working its way across her face.

"You moved. I'm almost done. Gut thing your hair is fine. If it was thick, it wouldn't fit under your kapp." She tied it off and twisted the braid to form a bun.

Anna placed her fresh new kapp over her head and smiled. "I'm ready."

"And none too soon. I hear Mamm calling."

"Let's go."

As they walked down the stairs, Abe appeared, handsome in his new attire—boots shining and bow tie crisp. He looked up at his future bride and smiled. She was a sight to behold. Fresh and lovely. God was blessing him abundantly.

They walked out to the barn together. The weather had cooperated. It hadn't rained for several days and the pathway to the barn was dry. There was a slight breeze, but the sun predominated sending its warmth downward, almost as confirmation of this union about to take place.

The service was serene. Anna barely heard the words as her mind was filled with thoughts of her new life with Abe. The droning of the male voices and then the songs from the *Ausbund* melded into her consciousness but it was as a dream. She found herself standing before the minister facing Abe. He was looking deeply into her eyes. At last the minister took their hands in his and gave them the blessings and mercy of God. "Go forth in the name of the Lord. You are now husband and wife."

They stood a moment longer just embracing the significance of the words. Then holding hands they went and sat together as family members rose to offer their congratulations and words of wisdom. Anna caught sight of her mother, who was dabbing her eyes with a tissue. It was difficult not to add her own tears, but she felt strongly about it being God's will for this marriage to take place. She felt blessed indeed.

Chapter Thirty

Eventually, they began the reception. A table was set in a corner of the barn where the bride and groom were served first, along with her attendant, Beth. Anna had prearranged to have Josiah accompany her sister. Beth glared over once to show her disapproval, but she quickly got over it as Josiah and she began conversing. He was definitely the most interesting single man there, she reminded herself as she relaxed her body and joined in.

The children behaved well throughout the entire event, which surprised and pleased Anna and Abe. "See? Already they're adjusting," he said as they discussed it.

"They're having too much fun to cause a raucous," she said with a grin. "But for whatever reason, I'm relieved. Abe are you upset that so many people came?"

"Of course not. It's kind of people to want to share this day with us. I think it means a lot to everyone to see you smile once again."

"Jah, it's been a struggle. Denki for marrying me, Abe. I hope I'll be a gut wife and mudder for your kinner."

"Don't thank me, Anna. You're the one to be thanked. You're taking on a huge task. I'll be forever grateful."

"Not a task. It's a privilege to have that trust."

"Let's not get too serious. Come, finish up and you can introduce me to your guests."

Beth felt Josiah's eyes on her as she removed their plates and headed for the kitchen area. When she turned, he was standing a few feet away, his arms folded in front of him. "Beth, do you want to take a walk with me?"

"I guess so. I'm tired of sitting, that's for sure."

She didn't bother with her shawl since it had warmed up considerably since morning. They went out the front door and walked slowly around the drive. Several colorful patches of crocus brightened the landscape and the fresh greens of new grass permeated the air. It was almost spring and new life was apparent everywhere they looked.

"I love this time of year," she said, a smile lighting up her face.

"Jah, me too. Sometimes I wish I had taken up farming instead of carpentry. Then I'd be outside more."

"But you're so talented. You have to use the abilities Gott gave you."

"That's one of the things that convinced me to start my own business. I do feel I've been blessed. It's always been easy for me. What is your talent, Beth?"

"I don't have any."

"Not true. You're very schmaert. You pick up things real quick-like."

"Oh, I guess if you're talking about things at work. Jah, I find it pretty easy. But I could never learn Greek like you're doing."

"How do you know? Why not let me teach you what I know."

"Maybe. We'll see. I like to read about travel."

"Maybe you'll do mission work."

"Nee, I doubt it. I'll probably do what every other Amish maed does—marry and have a brood of kinner."

"You don't sound too enthusiastic."

"Actually, I'll be ready to settle down some day."

"Maybe I'll be around when that happens."

"Don't hold your breath, Josiah. I'm a hard one to predict."

He laughed out loud. "Jah, you can say that again."

They walked to the horse stable and went inside to pat the three horses her parents owned. Then after a few minutes they returned to the house.

Beth had to remind herself that they would never be a couple. Too much water over the dam. Or could they get past that and start over? She secretly hoped one day it might happen.

As many of the older women continued to set up the next round of platters and bowls of food, the younger girls cleared the tables from the first round of diners and placed silverware for the next group. It took a lot of coordination to keep things moving, but it went smoothly. Rose was encouraged to spend her time with the guests and she went around greeting and hugging her friends. She was surprised to see her friend from the next district, Mary Zook, with her husband, Leroy and her three girls. Mary and she had become good friends in a sewing bee, which had dissolved a couple years before.

"Well, Mary, look at you! Just as pretty as ever. You never change," Rose said as she took her friend's hands in hers.

"Neither do you!" They kissed and discussed the wedding. "Your Anna looks lovely. I'm so thankful she found such a wonderful-gut man."

"Jah, we're happy, too. And how are your dochders? I see Katie's expecting again."

"Jah, and she feared she'd be barren after her battle with cancer."

"How's she doing?" Rose asked.

"Real gut."

"Praise the Lord. And Ruthie and Emma look real happy. They're fine girls. I'm so glad Ruthie married an Amish man."

"And your Beth. Does she have a beau?"

Rose sighed. "Who knows. She's had men interested in her, but somehow it never works out."

"The right one will come along someday. The young man who sat with them looks like a nice Amish man. Is he the fellow who owns the carpentry shop?"

"Jah and he was quite smitten with Beth, but that seems to be off, though she works for him."

"Then it may not be over."

Rachel came running over and grabbed her grandmother's apron. "Excuse me, but Mammi, my bruders are being mean to me. They took my ice cream."

"I'll let you go, Rose. Try to come to our new quilt-ing bee when you can."

"I would like to, Mary, but I'm in two others now and I ain't got any more free time. Give my love to your family and denki for coming."

"My pleasure. Bye, Rachel."

Rachel gave a slight wave as she took her grand-mother's hand to lead her to the source of her prob-lems. By then, the boys had scattered and so she stayed close to Rose instead.

Abe stayed with Anna the whole time as she took him by the hand and introduced him to her friends and relatives. They didn't have a moment to themselves, but she was rather proud—something Amish are not supposed to feel—as she led him around as her new husband. She could tell by the glances of some of her friends that they saw him as an attractive Amish man indeed.

Food was ever-present and it seemed that as soon as one meal was completed, preparations began for the next one. Families and couples arrived and departed, but there was always a group of two or three hundred people in attendance at any one time. At one point, Anna had to sit and rest her weary feet. She removed her high leather shoes once and rubbed her sore toes. Abe smiled down at her. "I think you'll sleep well to-night, Anna."

"I expect so," she agreed, wondering if he was plan-ning to sleep on the sofa again.

"There you are." A girlfriend from school came over and patted her head. "I've been stopped a hun-dred times while trying to get over to you."

Anna introduced her to Abe and then several other

people joined their group. Anna replaced her shoes and stood up again. Then Abe went to get some cookies for them. Neither had eaten much due to nerves, but cookies were always easy to get down. Especially the chocolate chip ones.

In the evening, the singing went into full mode. The younger people sang lively songs from the past and a few paired off and sat close together as they sang. There'd be more weddings the following season—that was for certain.

Hopefully, Anna would return to attend some of them.

Eventually, people began to leave and by eleven, it was just her parents, Beth, and the bride and groom.

"I guess we'll turn in," her mother said, stifling a yawn. "It was nice, jah?"

"Wonderful. Denki for all you did, Mamm and Daed," Anna said as she removed her shoes for the night and leaned back on the sofa.

Abe sat next to her. "Jah, it was a beautiful wedding and reception. I can't thank you enough."

"And we had enough food," Isaiah said, rolling up his sleeves. "I was scared for a minute when I saw all those buggies heading our way."

"Amish never go hungry," Rose stated. Everyone nodded agreement.

"I ate too much," Beth said patting her stomach. "That filling was grand. Who made it, Mamm?"

"Several brought filling. We have some left over. We'll send some back with you to Ohio on Saturday," she said to Anna and Abe.

"Not if I get it first," Beth teased.

"Mercy, there's enough for five families," Rose said.

Beth stood and said good night and headed to her room. "We'll be busy tomorrow. It's a mess in here."

"Not too bad," Anna said as she looked around. "Many hands—light work."

"Jah, true," Rose said, fanning herself with a section of the Budget. "My age is catching up to me."

"You're still young," Isaiah said to his wife. "You could still have more kinner."

"Gott forbid! We'll leave that up to Beth and Anna."

Anna's face flushed and she looked down at her hands.

Her parents stood and said good night as they departed the room, taking a lantern with them. It left one for the newlyweds.

After they heard the bedroom door close behind her parents, Anna reached down to gather her shoes.

"Let's not go up just yet," Abe said softly. "It's the first time we've been alone and I'm afraid once my head hits the pillow, I'll be out till morning."

So he was planning to sleep with her. Good thing she had a double bed in her old room now. A twin size would be way too small. She laid the shoes aside and sat back in her seat.

He moved closer to her and took her hand. "It was a wonderful-gut day. You looked lovely, Anna."

"Denki."

"The kinner behaved pretty gut, don't you think?"

"Jah, they did, for the most part."

"You sure have a lot of friends and family."

"Jah."

"I know you'll miss them. I'm sorry."

"It's okay. I'll have your family and I make friends pretty easy. I also have Dinah and Hosea."

"That's right. I'm glad."

"Abe, I'll be so busy being a housewife and mudder, I won't have time to get lonely. Please don't worry about me." She placed her hand on his and looked directly into his eyes.

"May I kiss you, Anna?"

She nodded. He slowly pulled her over to himself and embraced her in his arms. He kissed her cheek and the side of her neck. Then he raised her chin and moved his lips gently upon hers. It was sweet and tender. It nearly brought tears to her eyes. Jah, he was a gut man. She knew in that special moment that she could learn to love this dear Amish husband of hers. It might not take as long as she had expected.

They rose together and walked to the staircase. As she walked up ahead of him, he made certain that the lantern shined on her path. He was a gentleman. He would wait for her to love him.

* * * * *

HARLEQUIN® LOVE INSPIRED®

Widowed single mom Rebecca Mast accepts carpenter Daniel King's offer of assistance in opening her dream quilt shop—but she isn't prepared for the bond he forms with her son. Will getting closer expose her secret—or create a new opportunity for love with her long ago friend?

Read on for a sneak preview of
THE WEDDING QUILT BRIDE by Marta Perry
available May 2018 from Love Inspired!

Chapter One

Two days after Rebecca Mast's return to her childhood home in Lost Creek, she walked down the lane of the family farm toward her future. Her black widow's dress contrasted starkly with the pale greens and bright yellows of a sunny spring day in the Pennsylvania countryside. Her son, six-year-old Elijah, trudged next to her, holding tight to her hand rather than skipping and hopping ahead down the lane like one of his cousins would.

It was early yet, she assured herself. Surely soon he'd forget the darkness of the past few years and be like any other Amish child his age. That was the heartfelt prayer of her heart for her son. As for her...well, the return to normal would take longer, if it ever happened.

But at least she was home, with her family around her, and today she would take the first step toward a new life for her son and herself. That alone was something to make her heart thankful.

The frame two-story house came into view ahead

of them, standing at the point where the farm lane met the country road. When her mammi had written that old Mr. Evans had gone to live with his daughter and put the house up for sale, she'd known exactly what she wanted to do with the money she'd receive for selling the farm she and James had owned in Ohio.

The down payment James's brother John had given her had been enough to cover the cost of the house. John's continuing monthly payments would pay to remodel the old place into a secure, peaceful home for her and Elijah, and the quilt shop she'd have in the downstairs rooms would support them. That was the extent of her dreams for the future, and it was enough.

Daniel King stood waiting by the back porch, leaning against one of the posts as if he could wait there all day for her, if need be. As they came closer, her stomach tightened as she searched the tall, broad figure for a glimpse of the neighbor boy who'd been her childhood playmate. She didn't find him, nor did she see the gangly teenager who'd told her all about his crushes on the girls in their rumspringa group.

Daniel had grown into a strong, sturdy-looking man. It was her own uncertainty that made her long to find something in him that was familiar. The rich, glossy brown of his hair was a bit darker now, and the fact that he didn't have the traditional Amish beard allowed her to see his stubborn jaw.

He'd always had that stubbornness. His golden-brown eyes had a glint of kindness that she felt sure reflected his kind heart, and his lips curled in a familiar grin. Her tension evaporated, and she smiled.

"Rebecca!" He came forward now to greet them, taking her hands in both of his for a momentary squeeze. "It's wonderful gut to see you again." His face sobered. "I'm sorry for your loss."

She nodded. She had a stock of reasonable comments to use when someone commented on her widowhood, but they didn't seem appropriate for Daniel, who'd known her so well.

Daniel didn't seem to notice. He'd focused on Lige, who was hiding behind her skirt, and he squatted down to eye level.

"You must be Elijah. I've heard about you from your grossmammi. She told me you just turned six. Is that right?"

Lige, clutching the fold of Rebecca's skirt, gave the smallest of nods. Fortunately, Daniel didn't seem to expect more.

"I'm Daniel," he said. "I live over there." He pointed across the field to the neighboring farm. "When your mammi and I were your age, we used to play together every day."

Still no response. She tried to think of something to say to pull his attention from Lige, but Daniel was already rising, his smile intact. "Ach, it's hard to get to know a lot of new folks at once, ain't so?"

"Yah, it is," she said, grateful for his understanding. "Sam tells me that your carpentry business is a wonderful success these days." Sam, Rebecca's older brother, had been best friends with Daniel's older brother, Caleb. It had seemed natural for her and Daniel to pair up, as well.

"Ach, I wouldn't say great, but it's doing okay. It doesn't give me much time to help Caleb with the dairy farm, but I do what I can. And he's got Onkel Zeb and young Thomas Stoltz to work with him, too."

"I'm sure he needs it, running such a big dairy operation." Daad had told her how Caleb had increased his herd until it was one of the larger ones in the valley. "I'd be most happy if you have time to take on this job for me."

She glanced at the house, trying to picture it the way it was in her dreams. With Daniel's help, that dream could be a reality.

"Let's go in and have a look at what you want done," Daniel suggested. He held out a hand as she reached the three steps up to the back porch. "Mind the treads, now. There's a loose board there I'll fix right off."

She nodded, turning to help Lige up to the porch. "It's a little bit run-down now," she told him. "But Daniel will help us turn it into a gut home for us."

Lige darted a cautious sideways glance at Daniel, but he still didn't speak. She tried to suppress a sigh. If she'd realized earlier the harm James's behavior was doing to Elijah…but what choice did she have? James had been his father, and there was no getting away from that.

The back door opened into the kitchen, and they stepped inside.

"The cabinets need some repair," Daniel said, swinging a door open and closed. "But they're good solid wood—none of those thin layers they use sometimes now."

Rebecca was busy picturing the kitchen with the cabinets freshly painted white and seedlings growing in pots on the wide, sunny windowsills. "The gas range is perfect," she said. "But I'll have to replace the electric refrigerator with a gas one."

"I don't know much about the electrics, but there's

a man I worked with on a few Englisch houses who does that kind of work. He could take out all the electric for you."

"Wonderful gut." Surely the fact that things were falling into place meant that her plans were in accord with the gut Lord's will. "Our table will fit in this space, won't it, Lige?"

He nodded, but hadn't yet let go of her skirt.

"When do your things arrive?" Daniel pulled himself out from behind the refrigerator, a cobweb clinging to his straw hat.

"In a few days." Smiling, she reached up to lift the cobweb away, inadvertently brushing his cheek. She withdrew her hand quickly, trying to ignore the way it tingled from the brief contact. "The family will store everything for us until we can move in here."

The back of the house held the kitchen, a pantry and two smaller rooms. One would be their living room and the other a storeroom or workroom. Swinging the door open, Rebecca stepped into the room at the front of the house. Her breath caught.

The room extended across the whole front of the house, and sunshine poured in through the windows to lay across the wide-plank floors. The back wall would be perfect for shelves, and she could have a display area of quilts on one side and stocks of fabrics and notions on the other.

"You look happy," Daniel said, his brown eyes warm. "Is this going to be your living room?"

"No." She swung in a slow circle, taking it all in. "This will be what I've been dreaming of. This will be my quilt shop."

She knew her happiness had to be shining in her

face. And when she looked at Daniel, she saw her anticipation reflected in his eyes, crinkling as they shared her feeling. There, at last, was her old friend.

***

Don't miss
THE WEDDING QUILT BRIDE by Marta Perry,
available May 2018 wherever
Love Inspired® books and ebooks are sold.
www.Harlequin.com

We hope you enjoyed this story.

If you love **inspirational**, **heartwarming** romances, be sure to look for all six Love Inspired® books every month.

*Widowed single mom Rebecca Mast returns to her
Amish community hoping to open a quilt shop. She
accepts carpenter Daniel King's offer of assistance—but
she isn't prepared for the bond he forms with her son.
Will getting closer expose her secret—or reveal the love
she has in her heart for her long-ago friend?*

Read on for a sneak preview of
THE WEDDING QUILT BRIDE
by **Marta Perry**,
available May 2018 from Love Inspired!

"Do you want to make decisions about the rest of the house
today, or just focus on the shop for now?"

"Just the shop today," Rebecca said quickly. "It's more
important than getting moved in right away."

"If I know your *mamm* and *daad*, they'd be happy to
have you stay with them in the *grossdaadi* house for always,
ain't so?"

"That's what they say, but we shouldn't impose on them."

"Impose? Since when is it imposing to have you home
again? Your folks have been so happy since they knew you
were coming. You're not imposing," Daniel said.

Rebecca stiffened, seeming to put some distance between
them. "It's better that I stand on my own feet. I'm not a girl
any longer." She looked as if she might want to add that it
wasn't his business.

No, it wasn't. And she certain sure wasn't the girl he
remembered. Grief alone didn't seem enough to account

for the changes in her. Had there been some other problem, something he didn't know about in her time away or in her marriage?

He'd best mind his tongue and keep his thoughts on business, he told himself. He was the last person to know anything about marriage, and that was the way he wanted it. Or if not wanted, he corrected honestly, at least the way it had to be.

"I guess we should get busy measuring for all these things, so I'll know what I'm buying when I go to the mill." Pulling out his steel measure, he focused on the boy. "Mind helping me by holding one end of this, Lige?"

The boy hesitated for a moment, studying him as if looking at the question from all angles. Then he nodded, taking a few steps toward Daniel, who couldn't help feeling a little spurt of triumph.

Daniel held out an end of the tape. "If you'll hold this end right here on the corner, I'll measure the whole wall. Then we can see how many racks we'll be able to put up."

Daniel measured, checking a second time before writing the figures down in his notebook. His gaze slid toward Lige again. It wondered him how the boy came to be so quiet and solemn. He certain sure wasn't like his *mammi* had been when she was young. Could be he was still having trouble adjusting to his *daadi*'s dying, he supposed.

Rebecca was home, but he sensed she had brought some troubles with her. As for him…well, he didn't have answers. He just had a lot of questions.

Don't miss
THE WEDDING QUILT BRIDE by Marta Perry,
available May 2018 wherever
Love Inspired® books and ebooks are sold.

LIEXP0418

Love Inspired®

Save $1.00

on the purchase of any
Love Inspired® book.

Redeemable at participating Walmart outlets.

Save $1.00

on the purchase of any Love Inspired® book.

Coupon valid until July 31, 2018.
Redeemable at participating Walmart outlets in the U.S. and Canada only.
Limit one coupon per customer.

52615199

5 65373 00076 2 (81000 12313

® and ™ are trademarks owned and used by the trademark owner and/or its licensee.

LICOUP0318WM

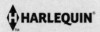
HARLEQUIN®

Save $1.00

on the purchase of any

Harlequin® series book.

Redeemable at participating Walmart outlets.

- ✂

Save $1.00

on the purchase of any Harlequin® series book.

Coupon valid until July 31, 2018.
Redeemable at participating Walmart outlets in the U.S. and Canada only.
Limit one coupon per customer.

52615203

5 65373 00076 2 (8100)0 12314

SPECIAL EXCERPT FROM

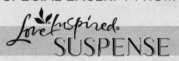

Love Inspired.
SUSPENSE

With her serial killer brother out of prison and on the lam, can Staff Sergeant Zoe Sullivan prove she's not his accomplice before it's too late?

Read on for a sneak preview of
BOUND BY DUTY by *Valerie Hansen,*
the next book in the MILITARY K-9 UNIT miniseries,
available May 2018 from Love Inspired Suspense!

She was being watched. Constantly. Every fiber of her being knew it. Lately she felt as though she was the defenseless prey and packs of predators were circling her and her helpless little boy, which was why she'd left Freddy home with a sitter. Were things as bad as they seemed? It was more than possible, and Staff Sergeant Zoe Sullivan shivered despite the warm spring day.

Scanning the busy parking lot as she left the Canyon Air Force Base Exchange with her purchases, Zoe quickly spotted one of the Security Forces investigators. Her pulse jumped, and hostility took over her usually amiable spirit. The K-9 cop in a blue beret and camo ABU—Airman Battle Uniform—was obviously waiting for her. She bit her lip. Nobody cared how innocent she was. Being the half sister of Boyd Sullivan, the escaped Red Rose Killer, automatically made her a person of interest.

Zoe clenched her teeth. There was no way she could prove herself so why bother trying? She squared her slim shoulders under her off-duty blue T-shirt and stepped out, heading straight for the Security Forces man and his imposing K-9, a black-and-rust-colored rottweiler.

Clearly he saw her coming because he tensed, feet apart, body braced. In Zoe's case, five and a half feet was the most height she could muster. The dark-haired tech sergeant she was approaching looked to be almost a foot taller.

He gave a slight nod as she drew near and greeted her formally. "Sergeant Sullivan."

Linc Colson's firm jaw, broad shoulders and strength of presence were familiar. They had met during a questioning session conducted by Captain Justin Blackwood and Master Sergeant Westley James shortly after her half brother had escaped from prison.

Zoe stopped and gave the cop an overt once-over, checking his name tag. "Can I help you with something, Sergeant Colson?"

Don't miss
BOUND BY DUTY by Valerie Hansen,
available May 2018 wherever
Love Inspired® Suspense books and ebooks are sold.

www.LoveInspired.com

Looking for inspiration in tales
of hope, faith and heartfelt romance?

Check out **Love Inspired®** and
Love Inspired® Suspense books!

New books available every month!

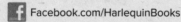